Tragically Hip, Twisted

Illustrated stories inspired by Hip songs

By David Sachs

(Includes "Lionized & Little Bones", named National Post Ebook of the Week)

This is the original work of David Sachs. No endorsement or involvement from the Tragically Hip is implied.

THE TRAGICALLY HIP WAY

KIN

About Tragically Hip, Twisted:

I have a strange hobby. I write short stories based on Tragically Hip* songs. Not the songs that tell a story – because they already tell a story. But the songs that don't quite. They're still evocative. They are emotionally nuanced and tell story snippets. The listener can piece together a multiplicity of possible stories from them.

I think this is part of the reason Gord has been so interesting as a frontman: the songs have this expressionistic character that he can interpret in different ways. In my stories, I pick one interpretation.

The first one I did was Locked in the Trunk of a Car, must have been 15 or more years ago. The others have been written over the intervening years. I've also had attempts at New Orleans Is Sinking; 50 Mission Cap; Wheat Kings; Are you Ready?; and Boots or Hearts – hopefully there'll be a second book some day. I'd especially like to do one of Courage: me covering the Hip covering Hugh MacLennan.

I've tried to take the feelings and contours of the songs from one medium to another – like Fantasia (or Courage). I listen to the song on repeat while I write: I hope the mood carries that way, and lyrics wind up in the narrative.

The stories stand on their own – you don't need to know the music. But for a unique musico-literary experience, I recommend listening to the respective songs, low, on repeat, while reading, just as I wrote it.

Or don't. It's a free country.

Links to download each story's foundational song are here:

www.davidsachs.com/TragicallyHipStories

I will also have a space for others to add their own interpretive stories of Hip songs online.

The Tragically Hip are Canada's house band. Their music has been the soundtrack of growing up for a generation of Canadians. Damn good band!

Half of author proceeds from this book go to cancer research.

Stories:

(For those keeping track at home, that's 4 from Fully Completely, 2 Day for Night, 1 each for Road Apples, In Violet Light and Trouble at the Henhouse.)

LOCKED IN THE TRUNK OF A CAR

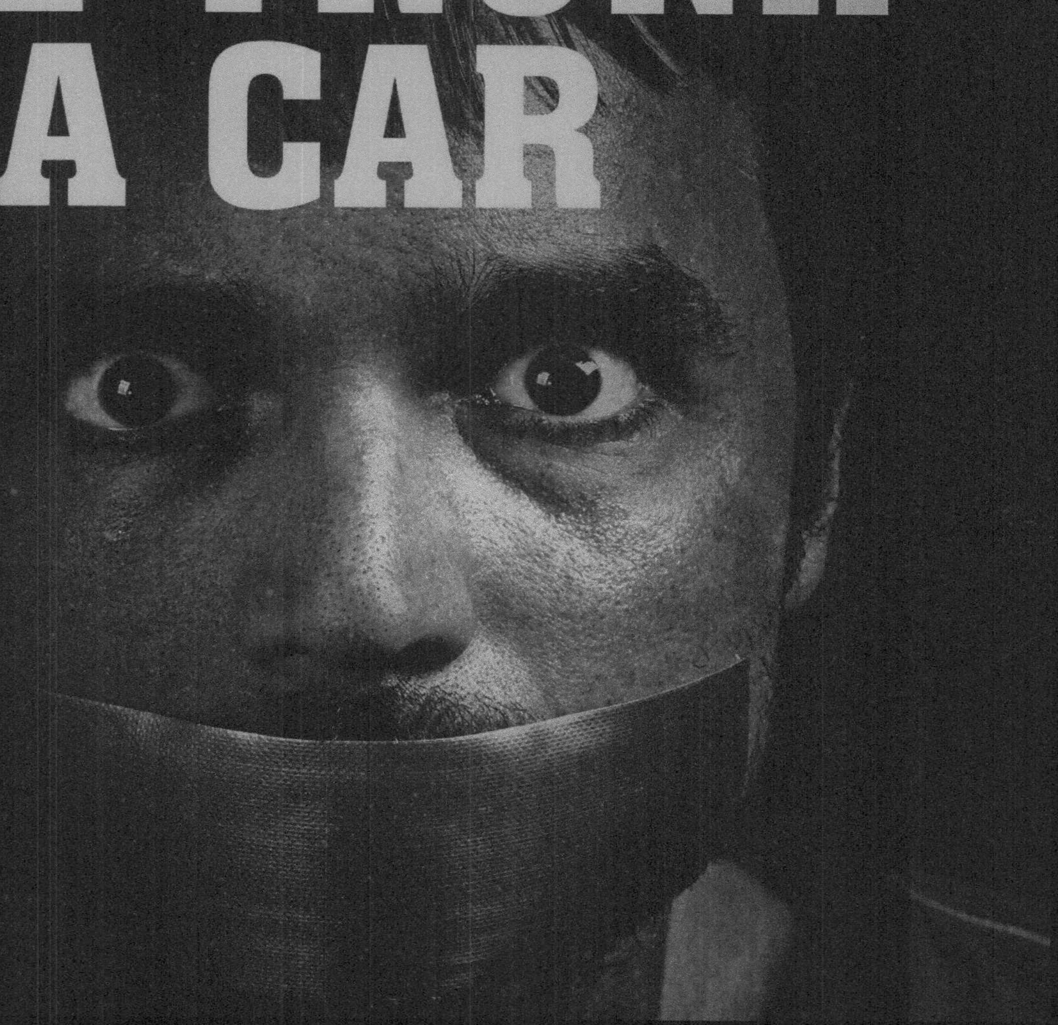

Locked in the Trunk of a Car, 1st variation

(album: Fully Completely)

I've woken up before in strange places, on couches perhaps, or with a girl in a strange bed, sometimes even in different cities. It's usually after a night of heavy drinking. There's that moment where you don't know where you are. It's disconcerting to wake into a completely new environment. It's like you've woken to a new world, an Alice-in-Wonderland type experience. It only lasts an instant usually, wondering where you are, but it seems much longer as your brain tries to make sense of your surroundings. I like that moment of uncertainty, between worlds.

This is different.

Waking in complete darkness like this, it lasts longer. It feels less like waking and more like you've just begun dreaming – the type where you know it's a dream and you can control your thoughts within the dream. That's what this feels like at first. Then, it slowly drips into the realization that I'm wrong, this is no dream. I feel my body, the tape, the pain. I kick my bound legs out and shake myself around. I can feel the duct tape across my mouth now, the throbbing in my head. I've been hit on the head. I know where I am. I'm locked in the trunk of a car. I don't know why. I don't remember – I know I was at dinner, then I was walking home. That's it, as far as I can remember. I don't know even if there IS anything more to remember – if I was hit suddenly, or if there was more to the story but the concussion erased it. That's the funny thing about not remembering.

I assume I'm going to die. I've done things in my life that have made people mad. I know there are people who want me dead. I don't know who's taken it upon themselves. So I'm waiting; there's nothing else to do.

I had a friend who knew he was going to die. The doctor gave him six months and the sonofabitch was right on the money. So my friend had this period in his life where he knew his own end. He lived, boy; he enjoyed that time. He spent it the right way, doing all the things people would figure they would do in that situation: fulfilling some of his dreams, spending time with the people he cared about, letting them know everything he wanted to tell them, all those things. I think we all have an instinctive desire, before we die, to say everything there is to say, everything we think or know. He had that chance. When you're dying, nobody makes fun of you for talking about the things that matter. It wasn't all Hallmark. He got laid. He did it right. This is different.

For a few minutes I argue with myself, trying to bring hope into the equation. I mean, I don't know who did this, I don't know what this is about. Maybe they're not going to kill me. But they are. I know it. Like my friend, I know my own end. But what good is that knowledge to me? Should I be living my life differently now that I know my time is measured? Should I be squeezing the juice out of every last second of life, making the most of this precious gift? Bound and gagged in the trunk of a car? My options are limited. My life, what remains of it, is playing out in my mind, in the dark. My body might as well be dead already.

I hear a door close, and feet shuffling; somebody's walking closer. I try to move to make noise, to get his attention, but I'm so confined I can just limply tap the side wall with my feet. It feels so impotent. Then the car door opens and I know that whoever it is doesn't care. He knows I'm here already. He's here to kill me probably. At least something is happening now, at least there's more than my brain to listen to. The car is started, we're going somewhere. Heh-heh. I wonder what my ultimate destination is. I'm scared now.

***

Car. Body. Me. My work is simple. I laugh about it as I start the car. I don't think about the body specifically. It's simple work if you don't think about it. Anyways, it needs doing right now. The garage is dark and ugly and it always makes me feel kind of spooked, but pulling out, the sun is up, and we are on our way into a beautiful day. Me, car and body. The Unholy Trinity, rolling down the street, on the way to our day job just like everyone else this morning. Rush hour traffic in Toronto I can do without. Everyone's got a place to go, though. I find this amusing. I know what I've got in my car. Hey buddy, what have you got in yours? What's in your trunk? Ha. Who knows? Who knows how many sick bastards are running around in this city with bodies in their trunks? Look at my car, green Chevy Caprice. Old and rusted. In Toronto rush hour it looks different from the Audis and Civics and SUVs, but nothing too peculiar about it. Maybe every car has a story as interesting as this. Every window has something behind it. I have a long drive; I don't think too much about the body specifically, just let my mind wander.

The traffic is murder. The Don Valley Parkway in summertime construction. I've got all day, though. It's nice when I'm not in a rush. I feel like I get paid to just sit in traffic and do nothing. I wish that was all there was to my job. I guess I shouldn't complain about the traffic then. It always ends eventually, and then there's that other part.

North of Toronto, I pull in at a truck stop for breakfast. I've been here enough times before, but nobody knows me. The regulars seem to talk to each other, to the waitresses, so easily. I eat in anonymity. It makes me uncomfortable. Everywhere is like this now. You cultivate anonymity in this job, you don't want to be noticed, right? But you feel like a ghost.

"'Scuse me, I'm heading up to ditch a body! Whereabouts are you from fella? Can I buy you a beer?" I want to shout.

I eat enough to fill my belly, know I'm alive. Too early for a beer anyway. I tip small, feeling angry at being unnoticed, then feel guilty after I've walked back out into the parking lot and the sun is back on my face and my belly is warm and full. It's not the waitress's fault things are like they are.

The car seat is nice and warm when I sit down. I need gas, put ten bucks in just to top off. Doesn't take too much gas. Not like these truckers, with their heavy loads, eating their weight in fuel to get where they're going. My load isn't so heavy in that respect. I use my bankcard at the pump. No need to talk to anyone.

I wonder how four million people can live in the city and all pass through each other like ghosts. Or am I the only one? I guess it's all a matter of degrees.

***

It hurts, bouncing along the highway like this. Been in this position, all my weight on these few points, for a while. If you've ever passed out on a hard floor and slept the night in one position, you can begin to understand what I'm talking about. The pain gets so bad in your shoulders and hips, but you kind of get used to it after a while. After a while, anything can become background noise. Then the funny thing is I can think about other things, forgetting the pain, but remembering again when we stop.

When the bouncing stops and I'm suddenly still, it feels like the pain is leaking from my body. I can't think about anything else but my shoulder, all swollen up and leaking pain. After that pain passes, I finally process the fact that we've stopped. The car is quiet. And there are others out there moving slowly. I can hear cars. A parking lot, or a gas station or something. I try to bang on the side of the trunk but I just can't get any force, I can't do anything more than tap. I try to bang my head against the side, but I can't get any traction; my shoulder slips a little on me. My god, I can actually hear people talk. How can they not hear me? My heart sounds so loud, my nose-breathing is so heavy, for God's sake, how do they not hear me? The duct tape muffles my voice as I try to scream, but they should be able to still hear something. Why can't I tap any harder than this? This could be my only chance and I'm so impotent. How can they not sense that there is a human being here, feet away from them, with just this thin sheet of metal separating us? I'm here!

I recognize his footfalls, his feet shuffling back over the gravel of the parking lot. His key is in the door. We're going to move again. We're going to leave here and he's going to kill me, and these people are standing here close enough to fucking smell me. Oh God, I'm RIGHT HERE. Why can't I tap any harder than this? The car is started. Please, there's so little time left, and this is my whole life. We're moving again. No. Stopped again. What… he's getting gas. I can't keep tapping, it hurts too much, my calves feel like they're burning. Let him gas up in peace. He knows I'm here.

Back onto the highway. I wonder if there is any good way to run out a life without a body? I wonder if there is any good way to run out life at all? Maybe the whole point of life is not thinking about when you're gonna die. Maybe, once you know you're dying, the game is over. Maybe it wasn't all so satisfying for my friend, all those things he did in his final months. Maybe he was really dead already, he was just going through the motions. Maybe when you know you're dying, life is like scoring goals after the other team has pulled the goalie. Is that what it felt like to accomplish those things? In baseball, they don't let you bat in the bottom of the 9th if you've already won the game. Life's not like this. You keep going, scoring meaningless runs. Maybe I'm lucky, my body's been put on the injured reserve, I get to watch the clock run out from the bench, don't have to bother with meaningless exertions and Kabuki dancing. We're off the highway now, onto a smaller road.

Going slower, the vibrations change, become, like, deeper, hurts more. It's ironic. My body is so useless to me, all I've got left to live with is inside my mind, but I can't think straight with this FUCKING PAIN IN MY SHOULDER. Why can't I stop caring about the pain? I'm dying, why should pain be a concern for me?

We've made several turns. There's less noise now. We must be out of traffic, maybe in the country now, we've been gone so long, and we're going so much slower now. Turn again. This is a dirt road. This is it.

***

It's nice here. If it weren't what it is, this would be a place I would like to come to. I'm probably the only one who knows about it. I could show it to people. It would be my spot, where I could take friends or girlfriends, or anybody, for camping or swimming, or picnicking. But it is what it is. And what it is is where I dump the bodies. It's simple. Time to work.

I always back the car in. It's kind of tight down this lane through the brush. Hard enough to walk around the car without getting my arms cut up by these

20

thorns, wouldn't want to carry the body around. No room to turn the car around after either.

Grab the bag and weights from the back seat and carry it around back. What's that noise? That's the trunk. Oh shit.

***

"Don't move or I'll blow your head off."

I scream so hard my whole body feels like it will pop, but the duct tape mutes it, so that it is loudest in my own head. The light blinds me; I can't see anything. It takes a moment to calm, I don't know why; opening the trunk set off this wave of terror inside me, I started screaming, and then that voice.

Nothing more is said. My eyes are squinting straight up above, and slowly a very large handgun forms out of the white light. It's a foot or so from my face. There is a man holding it, a large man in jeans and a long-sleeved shirt.

"You're supposed to be dead."

I can't reply, but I think he gets the gist of what I would say. I'm not.

"Somebody fucked up," he says, "Fuck. FUCK. I HATE doing this. Why does this shit always happen to me? …Heh. I suppose I must look very selfish complaining. You're probably having a far worse day. And you've still got the killing to go through. This won't be easy for either of us, I guess."

He leans back from the car, and tucks the gun back into his pants. Looking around for a moment, he turns and drops so that his butt sits on the edge of the trunk, his back to me. His body partially blocks out the sun from my eyes.

"I'm not a killer," he says, "I'm sorry to have to do this to you." But his voice doesn't sound sorry at all.

"I'm just supposed to take care of the bodies. They know I don't do this kind of work," he turns and looks back at me, like he's angry at me. "Don't think I can't do it and I'm not gonna do it. Believe me, you're a dead man. I just mean, I'm not SUPPOSED to do it."

He turns back. Part of my mind is desperately searching for a way to escape, but I'm taped up in so many places. There's no way out unless he lets me.

"I've been involved before with killing. I just don't DO it, I mean, as a matter of course. It's not part of the job description. 'Course, life is tough all over, isn't it? Look at you. You're wrapped up like a Christmas present waiting to be opened. Only, 'opened' for you means deaded, know what I mean? Now that's really a rough job…. Fuck."

He gets up and begins walking around. Looking up out of the trunk, I can see thick trees around us, spruce and elm mostly, with wiry looking bushes poking around them. It's humid out, and I have the feeling we're next to water. Maybe it's because I know what comes next.

"It makes it hard to go back to the city after you kill someone," he continues, "That's the thing I really hate. There's always a first person you have to talk to. No matter how much you try to avoid people, eventually you gotta talk to someone. There's always a first person you have to talk to after killing somebody. And all you can think is, you poor fucking schmuck, do you realize I just killed somebody? Would you stand there so calmly and sell me my lotto ticket if you knew? But you actually feel like they do know something. They look at you, like you've got a mark on you. I don't talk to people much anyways… It feels like it's getting harder all the time. But these days are the worst. Go to a bar. Everybody's having a good time, guys are picking up girls, they've got clever things to say, they do clever things that they can talk about in clever ways – it's like they've got this secret they're all in on, this club I can't get into.

"I don't talk to anybody. I sometimes wonder how human beings can ignore somebody right in front of them, but I sit there in this place where everybody's talking to everybody, and nobody talks to me. They see me. I'm right fucking there. But nobody talks to me. And I feel like I can't open my mouth to talk, 'cause the words are just going to fall out and announce everything before I can stop them. I don't know why I go to bars at all."

I am suddenly aware of how wide open my eyes are. I realize that this is what terror looks like. It's funny because you don't even know you're doing it while you're doing it. It's one of those things.

"It doesn't matter. People have to be killed. It's no different from dumping the cargo, I just have to handle it properly first, right? My name is Pat, by the way. I'll be your killer this afternoon. Heh. Wish you could look around a little, buddy; it's nice here. This is my spot, I never get to share it with anyone but dead people."

He looks at me suddenly, and then walks back over. Reaching in, he grabs me by the front of the shirt, then his other hand goes over behind my head and pulls. Oh God no! AAAH! Fuck. He puts me somehow leaned back against the open trunk lid. My legs are below me, splayed out a little to the right. It hurts like hell. But I see what he means, it is a nice spot. It's wooded, dark and shaded, except the little spot where the car is. There's a little shaded path right down to the water. No sign of anything human as far as I can see. Just us.

"There. Now it's our spot. It must give you some satisfaction seeing where you're gonna, you know, be… I'm sorry, I don't know why I said that. I have no fucking idea what's satisfying to you right now or not. Hey, you want a cigarette?"

He turns and – oh God! AAAAAAARGH! The tape is ripped off my mouth in one motion. I can't stop screaming.

"Well, I don't blame you. You've got a lot to scream about, but there's no one can hear you anyways, so scream if you need to. Just don't freak out or anything."

He pulls the pack of cigarettes from his pocket and sticks one in my mouth. It stops my crying. Like a baby and a pacifier. I blink away some tears and watch him lower the lighter to me. I breathe and the cigarette lights right away. It was so windy last night, I remember, but there's no wind now, at least not here. Just humidity.

"I figure, what the hell. I never get to talk to anyone in this job, you know, never can enjoy what I'm doing with the cargo, so why not make the best of things, right? I mean, what the hell. If you have to die, and I have to kill you, we may as well make it as, you know, I mean, we might as well just chill and at least relax and just enjoy where we are. Right?"

"Why are you killing me?" I ask out of the side of my mouth, kind of mumbled because of the cigarette.

"That's the job, buddy. I'm not supposed to, I'm just supposed to get rid of you, but here we are and what are we gonna do?"

"No, I mean, why am I here? Who is it that wants to kill me?"

"Look, I don't get into the business side of things. I just know what I've gotta do. I'm sure your job, not that I know what you do or want to know, but I'm sure you got things you gotta handle that you don't think about either. Everybody does."

"If you're going to kill me anyways, why can't you just tell me?"

"Because I'm telling you, I don't know anything about it! Don't you listen? I don't fucking know, okay? I'm just a delivery boy, okay? I'm not a boss of anyone… but I'd rather be in my position than yours right now, I'll tell you that."

A cigarette smokes fast when you can't pull it away from your mouth. I don't smoke actually, or I should say, didn't, but I guess it won't kill me at this point. My eyes are tearing up again from the smoke, though; I wish I could take the cigarette from my mouth for a moment to blow the smoke away.

He looks at me, and pulls the cigarette from my mouth. I exhale deeply and cough, closing my eyes to clear them up.

"Want more?"

"One more puff."

He gives it to me, then throws the butt down into the dirt and steps on it.

"I'll pay you to let me go," I say, "I'll pay you – whatever it takes to make it worth your while, I'll pay you."

"Yeah? Enough even to cover my funeral expenses? 'Cause that's what it'll be if I let you go. This isn't some volunteer job, buddy – you do what they tell you in this job. It's you or me, and between you and me, I pick me. No offense, I'm sure you're a hell of a sweet guy, and I'm sure you got a ton of people that'd miss you, but I'd sure as hell miss me, so that ain't gonna happen."

"Look, please, I know you don't wanna do this."

"It doesn't matter what I want to do. We all gotta do stuff we don't want to do, why should my life be any easier than anyone else's?

"We don't all kill people!"

It came out like a sob; I didn't like the way it sounded.

"Oh, like you're so fucking perfect! You're so fucking better than me. You know, I hate people like you, you think you're so superior. You don't know what my life is like. It could just as easily be you in this position, and if it were, you'd be doing the same shit as me. Don't judge me. What gives you the right?"

"Look, I'm not judging you, but –"

"You're already dead! Don't you get that? As soon as they put you in the trunk, you were already dead. Abandon all hope ye poor bastard who enters my trunk. They've killed you already, so, how about we just assume you're dead and put that behind us, and get on with our lives, I mean, you know, this conversation. Heh. I know that came out funny. Look, I just wanted to enjoy the fucking few minutes we could here and thought you'd fucking appreciate it, so don't try and ruin this for both of us, okay?… It's like, I can never tell anyone I talk to what I do, I always feel like I'm hiding something. I just thought, with you, we could just sit here and I wouldn't feel that way. You know, if you don't want to chill, I can just finish this conversation fast if that's what you'd prefer."

"No, no, look, it's cool. We'll just – we'll just chill for a minute… …So, umm… you got a girlfriend or anything?"

God, what the hell kind of question was that? I'm trying to think of anything to talk about. He doesn't look at me, just shakes his head. "No. No, you know, it's hard to meet people in Toronto. And like, I don't even know what kind of chick would want to be with someone who does what I do."

"So… your job makes things rough for you," God, if I can just get him talking like this, maybe he won't do this, maybe he'll not be able to kill me if he talks to me, maybe he'll decide to retire, maybe he'll die of old age, I don't know, I just have to keep him talking. At least I'm alive while we talk.

"No, it's not the job exactly. I mean, there's a lot worse jobs. But it's the… it's society, you know? …It's like, there's two sides of society, the clean people and the dirty people. And once you become a dirty person, you can never be with the clean people again. It's so hypocritical, you know? I mean, nobody wants to be on the dirty side, but people just wind up there. I mean, I made my own choices. But I didn't start out doing this. I mean, I was a bartender at first. Wrong bar, that's all. It was a gang bar. Bad guys. It was cool to me, getting to see the underside of the city, of life. I was like a voyeur. It was like, I had a club that I was in on for once. Eventually, if you work with dirty people, you become dirty too. You start as a clean guy who gets to see the dirty side, you don't know that makes you dirty too, because once you've seen it, they've got you, they can't let you go. They'll pull you in and you can't say no and you become dirty too. I bet you wondered, how do people get these dirty jobs? Did their guidance counsellors give them some bad advice somewhere? Nah, it's just, you're in for a dime, you're in for a dollar. After a little while working there, I started to get scared about the whole thing. I prayed they wouldn't ever ask me to do more than serve drinks, you know? Because if they did, how do you say no? Then when they ask, they say it's just one little job. Just do this, and it's over. But this kind of job is never over. Instant career for life. Because every job connects with another one, and once you've done one job, you're expected to be in all the way, you don't stop. This job… never… ENDS… and when that's your job, you can't ever go back to clean people again. That's the way society is… How can I have friends outside now? How can I have a girlfriend? Nobody would

27

be with somebody like me. Yeah, I'll say to her, 'How was your day at school today, honey?' 'Oh, not bad. The kids behaved for once. I had to coach the girls' soccer team afterwards 'cause Vickie was sick. How was it for you today? You get the cargo out alright?' 'Oh, yeah. Took him up to the spot. Thank God he was dead! Just loaded him up and dropped him down.' 'I love you, jellybean.' 'I love you too, pooky-boots.'… Doesn't quite sound right, eh?"

"If you hate it so much, why can't you quit?"

"You can't quit! I just told you."

"Look, I know that before, when you still, you know, were clean, they couldn't let you go 'cause you might be dangerous, but now that you're dirty too, why can't you just walk away? They know that they have no reason to worry about you blabbing or anything."

"Yeah, well, that's just it. I'm dirty too, now…it's too late. What would be the point? Where am I gonna get a straight job? How do I explain what I've been doing all these years? Big blank space on the CV. Always looks bad. And how could I be with any clean people anyways? I couldn't tell them what I've done. You can't change what you've done, everybody knows that, that there are certain paths that your life takes and you can't undo it or make it go away."

"Well, for god's sake, Pat, learn to lie! It's not like it would be the worst thing you've done. Wouldn't it be better to live a lie than keep on like this? You can still get out, that's all that matters."

"What's the point?! What's the point of finding a good woman, and falling in love with her and having her fall in love with you, if it's a lie? Fuck it! Everyone in Toronto is so fake. I don't want to be fake. Look at you, with your designer shirt,

28

and your expensive watch. Would you let me marry your sister?"

"Well, it would be kind of awkward, to be quite frank…"

"Oh, that's very funny wise guy. Wise dead guy."

"Look, just… maybe I could help. I'll do anything I can to help you get your life sorted out. If we just calm down, we can figure this out."

"Shut up!"

His fist shoots out fast, right through my chin, and my body collapses back down into the pit of the trunk.

"You'd be just the same as everybody else if I knew you in different circumstances. Do you think YOU wouldn't look down your nose at me? Don't try and play games, talk about how you could help me. If I weren't going to kill you, you'd never talk to me at all… …look, I'm sorry I hit you, I lose my temper sometimes, let me help you back up."

"No! No, this is better. It really hurts my legs to sit up like that, just let me lie back here like this."

"Suit yourself."

"Look, Pat, I know it's none of my business … but this is your life you're talking about here. You only get one life, and if it's a bad one, and you know it's not what you want, how can you just let it keep going like that and do nothing to change it? Don't you see that you're wasting your life? Because one day, it's gonna be all over, and that's it. That will have been it."

I've always been a smooth talker; it's gotten me out of trouble many times. And into trouble just as many. I'm sharp, and this guy is dumb, and that's my chance.

"Yeah, well…" he says.

"Look at me! I'm in a position where I know a little of what I'm talking about here. I mean, I'm a dead man, that's what you said. I know what it feels like to know what the rest of your life looks like. And you can see the whole rest of your life as easily as I can. Only yours isn't limited in time like mine. Yours is limited because you won't let yourself out of this trap, and you can see yourself in it forever. But if this isn't the life you want, and you know that as much as you know anything, you have to just leave it! Now! No option is worse than continuing with what you already know is a failure. Just leave Toronto. Never go home. What have you got to go home to, Pat? Just go, and start a new life."

"Don't be ridiculous. This IS my life… I've lived here all my life, every… everyone I know is here, all my –"

"For God's sake, Pat, what kind of life is it? You feel sorry for yourself every day. You tell yourself this stupid idea that you took one wrong turn, and that's it, you're on the dirty side now and it can't be helped. Well I've got news for you, you can retake your life anytime you want. There's a right turn waiting for you to take it every single day. You said before that it was just your situation; I'd be just as dirty if I was in your place. But you can change your place, change who you are, and then this won't be you. You can prove it's not you. It's always scary to change, but it's so important. You can take that right turn like pulling off a Band-Aid, you just do it – don't be afraid, don't think about it, just have the balls and do it. Change everything, just like that."

"Look, do you think I'm gonna do something just because you say I don't have the balls to do it?"

30

"You don't have the balls! You're a pussy! You can leave anytime you want and you know it. It's just easier to feel sorry for yourself, to blame all your problems and your loneliness on this idea that you got dirty. Because then you don't have to make any effort, you can ride out your life being miserable without trying. Imagine how hard life would be if you were clean. To talk to people as equals, clean people, and enjoy life as much as they do. That's what you're afraid of. You're afraid of still being lonely and miserable and people not liking you and not having any excuse for it."

He steps away from the car and I can hear him shuffle his feet in the dirt as he leaves my field of vision. All I can see is the sky, and the sun, which is setting further by the minute, and the treetops, which lean over into the circle of my vision.

"Where could I go?"

Oh my God. He's listening.

"I don't know, Pat. There's a whole world out there that you've never explored. Once you make that decision to leave this miserable life behind, you can have just about any new life you want. You can shape it, choose ANY-thing. You could go east, and become a lumberer or fisherman. You could go west and become a, umm, become a... a ski instructor," why the hell did I say that? Ski instructor? Jesus. "If you earned some money, you could – you could go to Cuba and live there. Do you know how far a dollar goes in Cuba, Pat? There's no reason that life can't be yours. Who could stop it from happening if you just left right now? What would you do, if you could start your life now with a blank slate?"

"Yeah... ...Yeah... ...Yeah, you're right! I could just go. I could just... take another turn today and start everything fresh."

His voice is different somehow. It really sounds like another person.

"Leave everything," I say, "Just go."

He keeps talking like he doesn't hear me.

"I can leave everything. I'm strong, I'm smart, I can survive anywhere I go. And if I just go and survive, none of this will matter – it was just the way it was here. Eventually, I'll be so far from all this that it won't even be real anymore. It won't even be me anymore. I could make a completely new start and really be clean."

"That's right… that's right, Pat."

He's quiet for a moment, standing off on the side out of view.

"I'm gonna do it."

Oh God, why am I getting even more terrified now? Why is it scarier when you have a chance?

"I'm gonna do it... But I *can't just leave you*, buddy."

I stop suddenly. I forget to even breathe until my chest starts to burn. I don't say anything, he doesn't say anything for a moment, and I still can't see him.

"Pat, please, just… just leave me here, you know? Throw me out of the trunk, and just take the car and go. Do it now."

"I'm not taking the car. I'm not taking anything. The car is too dangerous. Who knows who'll be looking for it? And I don't want it. I want to do this right; I don't need it, not anymore. I'm starting everything over. And you're too dangerous too."

"Oh God, please Pat, I don't even know where you're going. I don't even know who brought me to you."

"Yeah, but somebody out there does, and if you're back, they'll come after me. You might go to the police, too. No, there's way too many ways you can fuck me. There's a million reasons I can't let you go, and there's only one reason against that. Because you changed my life. But I was gonna kill you before, so why should any of this change it? You were dead when I found you. And even if there weren't a million ways you could be dangerous to me alive, this was the job I took, and I've got to finish it. I can finally finish this job. I've got to walk away clean."

I see him then above me and he looks down at me. His face is actually calm, placid.

"Goodbye."

The trunk slams shut above me.

"Oh God, Pat! Pat, don't do this to me!"

I hear his feet shuffle and twigs snap around his body. Then I feel a clunk. The car starts moving, but no engine.

No, Pat. No, Pat. Please, don't do this. I can feel the car rolling down the hill. Pat, I can feel the car lurch with each of your clumsy footsteps.

Oh God, the car is in the water now. I can hear the bubbling all around me, I'm falling to the back of the trunk, it's sinking lower. Let me out! Oh God, don't let me watch my life drip away so slowly, with nothing but my own screams, I can't take it! Please, the water is coming in now. Let me out! *LET ME OUT!*

The End

LIONIZED

Lionized

(album: Fully Completely)

Cold wind blowing over my private parts. That ends the hot of the hot tub before I have both feet out. I bend over and take a snowy blast right in my wet butthole. Pick up the lighter and one-hitter and weed baggie and the towel, can't stop to dry, just throw it over my head and get to the patio door as my wet hair already starts to freeze.

It's locked. I forgot. This lock used to slip sometimes. Then it was fine for a while. Until tonight. Maybe the multiple tens-below-zero cold has something to do with it. I'm not here to do experiments. I just want to be on the hot side.

But I've already locked the other doors for the night.

The kids are asleep. I have the kids for the weekend. The cat is looking up at me from the other side of the sliding glass door. Wiseass.

I dry off, and wrap the small towel around my shoulders as best I can while I consider. At least it's a dry cold. I think that's the official tourist slogan for Quebec.

Worst case, I can wait in the hot tub till the kids wake up. Till the kids wake up and freak out that daddy's gone. This is probably the kind of parenting that leaves a mark. Pretend I was playing hide and seek. Maybe I'll tell the boy that, when I get to his window: "Wake up! We're playing hide and seek. Come and find me at the front door." He sucks at hide and seek. He hides in the same place every time and always gets distracted when he's seeking.

I'll have to wake a kid.

I'll scare the shit out of the poor kid. The poor boy. It'll have to be the older one, of course. The girl couldn't open the door. She is truly useless to me now.

Logistics are not simple. The house is a bungalow, but at the front, the ground level drops, and the boy's window is way out of reach. The snow is three feet deep, but even if it could support me, the window would still be too high. How will I reach the boy's window? If I bang and scream from here, I might wake the boy, but it probably would be moot since the neighbours would have the police and fire department and family services here by then. It's late, late, and a big screaming scene won't do.

I have to make it to the garage and see what resources I have there.

There's a good distance of snow to cross between the patio and the driveway. So let's go for it. I'll get some speed up on the deck and make it over that snow like Jesus on water.

One step, and I'm on my back. Oh. That is a hard deck. Everything in me is rocked. I'm so stunned I can't move for a moment, even with my naked flesh freezing to the iced deck. I roll onto one shoulder. The cat is laughing at me, in her inscrutable way. Fuck you, Mermaid the Cat. I push myself up. This time I slide and shimmy to the edge of the deck, towards the driveway. My feet burn. I wonder when frostbite amputation becomes part of the conversation. The towel hangs down my back like a cape. The towel is the kids'. It's blue, with a pouch at one corner that goes on the kids' head and makes a lion face. I wear the lion face on my head, but the towel is not quite big enough for my frame, which has been called disgusting.

The ice skin on the snow glimmers in the moonlight. It's beautiful. I test the snow-crust with one foot, and it holds. I lean further and it collapses. This is a terrible event, even in the context of this whole episode. The ice is a good half-inch thick, and it breaks jagged and sharp. I fall through it all, right up to dick level. The

40

pain distracts you for a second from the cold. And by you, I mean, me. But then the cold wins out, and you're like, holy shit, that's cold. That would be a good name for a law firm. Jagged and Sharp. Not Dick Level. Dick Level would be a good name for a rock band.

It feels like an icy hand has emerged from the snow and grabbed my testes; I must free my nuts immediately. I can't quite get my legs out of the hole. It's a full-body exercise. I don't excel at that kind of thing. I lean forward onto the ice and it holds under my distributed bulk for almost a second. I feel hope, and I swear, I smile. The crust compresses just a few inches, and I can half crawl my knees out of the first hole. The stupid lion towel catches some wind and spins around my head, so that it hangs down off the side of me. The lee side, of course.

Crawling, I have to keep as much of my body flat as possible to distribute the weight on the ice crust. I have one hand balled in a fist around the one-hitter and the lighter and the baggie, so the knuckles take all my weight, and scrape badly on the ice.

If you had to devise a challenge to stop people from advancing from A to B, I would recommend this. Not only is the enterprise as painful as one could imagine, but it seems so hopeless all the while. The shovelled area at the driveway seems to be getting further away. And why is the lion blue anyway?

If this were punishment for all the bad things I've ever done in my life, I would say, fine. Have at it, you win, God. But if it isn't, then what the fuck, God? Why did you have to pull this on me? Lesser men would have stopped and cried until the neighbours heard. Lesser men are probably on better terms with their neighbours, too.

The blue mane blows in the wind, and my arms are too busy to fix it. I am naked against nature. The lion king of the domain of ice and snow. I know why the lion is blue. He was bred for this.

Fuck those salesmen who walk on broken glass. Fuck those housewives who run across hot coals. Fuck those Iranians who whip themselves with metal spikes in that festival. Fuck every woman who's given birth, every man who's pissed a kidney stone, every marathon runner or extreme fighter. This is tough.

I'm almost to the driveway. At the snow's edge, it forms a crest towards me, like a wave above my head. The frozen imprint of the snowplow's curve. I have to get up and over. I push myself up with my legs, splayed out like a frog. I grab the lip with my elbows. I feel like one of those inspirational people with no hands who can accomplish ordinary tasks. I can't describe the physical gyrations it takes to get over that crest, but I think I went butt first, because that's how I land, down five feet onto the frozen gravel.

Naked, on the ground, my body arches in pain and I howl at the moon. The towel flies around me as I do my horizontal pain-dance, and I realize its frozen to my head. I get to my feet and make for the garage. First step, and I'm thrown to the ground. Don't do that again, God tells me. You don't feel any cushion from the ice on the gravel. Everything is covered in an inch or two of ice from the thaw and freezing rain and refreeze. I get up much more slowly this time. I am like the Borg, I learn from each setback.

I inch my way to the garage door. Now this is the life! I laugh out loud. Too easy. By the garage door I reach down and feel the ice that has taken hold on my balls and in my ass. Oh, to be a smooth-balled man! Oh Julie, you ruined my life, but you were right that I should have waxed my butt.

I grasp the door handle just inches off the ground and pull. My frozen fingers fail and I fall back onto the ice, with tremendous angular momentum. I close my eyes in the pain. I feel like I'm floating in pain. But no, I am, actually, drifting slowly on my back on the ice. I open my eyes, and things begin moving more quickly. The driveway is about 90 feet uphill to the garage. Or downhill to the road, and I'm over the lip. I turtle on my bare back, my feet are in the air, my arms flailing at the ice as I gain speed.

On the bright side, I'm not worried I'll hit traffic at this hour. On the down side, I realize just before I spill onto the road, that the road has been sanded. Fresh grit and gravel. I actually get air from the bump at the end of the driveway. I hit the road and my body starts flipping, either from the sudden change in friction, or my instinctive desire to get the hell off the ground. I have too much momentum and I slide, flip and fly into the opposite snowbank in baby-delivery position, my head on the road, my feet up high in the stirrups. The corner of the towel, I notice, is grasped in my hand. Wrapped across my back like this, from hand to head, it has protected me. A bit. I can feel the difference between my unscathed upper back and the horribly mistreated lower back and ass area. It feels momentarily nice to cool it in the snow bank. Then it doesn't.

Getting out is awkward. Walking across the street is slow and painful with the grit. I feel more impressed by the salesmen and the crushed glass.

Looking up at my driveway, I know I can't attack directly. It shines magnificently in the moonlight, an ice slide of solid silver. I have to try along the

43

side, dry-humping the dirty ridge of snow. The snow is more compact here from snowplowing so that it's easier to stay on the surface. The angle of it, and being able to crawl the edge with one leg over each side, having branches or bushes to grab; I like how I'm handling this. It's like, the yard was the marriage and this is the divorce. Sure, it sucks. But you can't help smiling when you think of what you were in before. And by you, I mean me.

I've been feeling sorry for myself a lot, helpless. Trapped in the current of the separation, the divorce, the situation at work. I've been eating too much. Smoking too much. Flabby of body, flabby of spirit. As I pass the lamppost, I glance down over my body. Red with abrasion, bleeding at the knees. Spotted with dirt and grit, ice clusters on the hairy spots. That big fat belly, and the big man tits. Perfectly adapted for my niche. Don't be fooled by that blubber, I'm pure animal savagery underneath. When I reach the end of my hump-ridge, I lean into the downslope and tumble to the driveway along the garage door. That's how I roll, now. I half crawl to the door handle. I use it to stabilize myself as I stand. I pull the handle more carefully this time. It's stuck. The garage door is frozen to the ground. I can't put much strength into my lift or I'll lose my grip, and I can't budge the thing. I have a full bladder now though, two beers worth from the hot tub. Ah, the hot tub. When this is all over, I'll have a hot tub.

I pee. It burns like hell. My penis is in no mood for this. I'll kill you, it screams, in a Mexican accent. I can pee from one corner of the garage door all along the ground to the handle. It trickles down to my toes. I try to shimmy further down to warm it all across, but my feet are too unsteady. I lower myself to my knees and edge my way along, my palms on the garage door, pee flowing away from the door around my knees. It feels good.

When I'm done, I crawl back to the handle. I bang the door with my fist a few times, and with my elbow. I again use the handle to come to my feet. I give it everything I have; the door swings up, my fingers come right off the handle, and I am back on my ass, down the hill, across the grit and gravel, and into the snowbank.

I start to cry. Why does this happen to me? Am I not fit to take care of myself? Am I so pathetic that I'm a danger to myself and my kids? Those poor kids. What kind of father would be here, naked, bloodied and pissed on in the snow, locked out of his home in the moonlight, a blue lion frozen to his head? Who else in the world does this happen to?

The awkward extrication. Back across the road, like a hot-footed salesman. Back humping the snowbank along the hill. It takes so long until I'm at the top, my mind wanders. I actually forget what I'm doing.

At the edge of Hump-Ridge, I look into the open garage and wonder, What did I want in the garage? Then I recall what's going on. I tumble down to the driveway and roll across and onto the dry concrete floor. It feels good. I remember the baggie and the one-hitter and the lighter, just by the door. I grab them. There is a wood step from the garage to the inner door into the house (which I know is locked). I stand on it.

Wood, it feels so warm on my feet. This is a poor man's hot tub. My hands are shaking so much, weed is flying away like pixie dust as I try to stuff my one-hitter. I finally get it filled and in my mouth, and my thumb is called upon to perform under deadly conditions to strike the lighter. How can the pain of one thumb be measured against the need of my whole body? Finally, flame. I bring it to the one-hitter, and breathe in deeply.

Let me tell you something: That is a sweet smoke. Oh, I never want it to end. As the perfumed cloud puffs out from my mouth, I try and pull it back in my nostrils. I take a second drag and finish the serving. I ash it out and fill it again. Then I try the door above me. Just for shits and giggles. Locked. It's not funny.

The ladder is at the back of the garage by the fireplace pipe. If there had been a fire inside, I could have snuggled against that pipe and warmed my cockles. I probably would have sliced my nuts off on loose sheet metal, but I'd take that chance. I grab the ladder and throw it over my shoulder, one arm through the slats. At the edge of the garage, I let the ladder tip down behind me and drag, letting it stabilize me as I cross a few feet of ice to the snowbank protecting the front of the house. I step up into the crusty snow to get some traction; I slide the ladder forward over the peak of the bank. Again, I climb. At the hump, I use the ladder to pull myself out from the crushed ice sheet and snow. My balls have actually gone beyond Absolute Zero. At this temperature, quantum effects reign and I can no longer say precisely where my balls have gone.

The ladder is a boon. You see right away why we have it all over the apes. Tools, motherfucker. It's awkward, but when I at last am crawling above the snow, I feel the blue lion flapping majestically behind me. The ladder is a bridge across the snowfield. It leaves red stripes on my knees and shins and palms as I crawl forward. At each ladder length, I dismount, break through the ice, sink into the crunchy cold stuff and pull the ladder forward. I pass under the girl's window.

May you never endure such pain, I say to my girl. Oh, I wish I were snuggling in bed with you, and not here. I'd rather be snuggling in bed with my ex-wife than here.

No. I'll take the cold.

At last I reach the boy's window. The ladder still prone on the snow, I stand on the last rung and look up. Too high by a few feet to reach. I know that manipulating the ladder vertically will require some stability and I prepare to launch myself feet first, balls deep.

A light hits my face and blinds me. I block it with my arm.

"Martin?"

It's the neighbour. Fifty feet away, across the leaf-bare trees. He tries to say my name the English way, but it comes out like mar-TAN.

There is a long pause. The wind strikes up around my legs, lifting the towel. I drop my hands away from my face to appear more dignified.

"Oui?" I say.

There is another long pause. I can't see him behind that light.

"Are you ok?" he says, like I'm too dumb to have this conversation in French.

"Yeah, I'm fine," I say. I can't stand this guy. He's right though, my French isn't that good.

"I 'eard some noise," he says.

"I was just in the hot tub," I say.

Yeah, I'm naked. Deal with it. It's fucking four in the morning, I can go naked to the hot tub if I want. I'm not the pervert out with a flashlight looking.

"Do you need help?" he says.

"Je suis bon," I say.

He's quiet, I'm quiet.

I can wait a long time, buddy. This is my element, and you're fucking freezing.

But he pushes it. He waits. I wait. The lion blows.

He shivers, I can sense it.

"Ok," he says.

"Yeah," I say. "À bientôt."

He goes back inside.

I'm overwhelmed with shame. Someday, his kids will tell my kids this story. The father shall be a disgrace and a humiliation and a burden to his children.

Why am I such a fuck-up? I look up at the boy's window. No, I won't wake you, my child, and scare you and ruin your dreams.

I make that decision with no recourse to fulfill it. But then I remember the trap door to the attic, in the ceiling of my bedroom closet. I can get to the attic from the garage.

I begin the journey back, with my ladder. I crawl, I dismount, and I move it forward. My woes are biblical. I am like some cursed protagonist from Arabian Nights.

When I must depart my Kingdom of Crunchy Snow for the Land of Ice and Body Slides, I am careful. I push the ladder down the snowbank, but force it through the icy crust so that it can support me as I lower myself, feet first this time. With my feet secure in the gravel and snow at the bottom of the snowbank, I pull the ladder free, using it again as a balance as I cross the icy drive into the garage.

48

From then, it is straightforward: I cross the garage like a biped, and lay the ladder against the back wall. I don't hesitate. I'm a father.

I climb the ladder, and hump myself over the truss stud into the loose fiberglass insulation of the attic. I cross the house in the dark. The insulation brings a new kind of discomfort, a stinging and itchiness. It is warmer here and I feel the throbbing of my extremities in the first stage of thawing. Hell's pain will be here soon, I know. I crawl across the insulation, climbing over each stud, keeping my head down below the points of the shingle nails that protrude from the low, angled roof just above. I can feel rodent turds: there is nothing else these pebbles and nuggets can be. I smell rotten dead varmints. I should really clean up here once in a while.

The trap door is a simple matter to open. I can get my fingers under a lip and as I pull it up, I am greeted by the warm light of my bedroom. I lie down on the frame and drop my legs through. Dangling from my waist, I let go. My legs cannot hold from the few feet drop, and I tumble backwards, knocking over shoes, landing in a pile of dirty laundry.

I get up and feel the full raw pain as my body reacts to the warmth and the blood begins to flow again. I collapse straightaway on my ass and cry.

After a minute, the pain has not subsided but I stand. I look in the mirror and see a monster: a red bloated, bloody pig of a man, with hollow dead eyes, and a blue lion on his head.

I walk to my boy's bedroom, gently open the door and approach his bed. I kiss him on the cheek and he stirs. I rub his hand and kiss his fingers.

I go next to my girl. She is facing the wall, and I roll her back and kiss her on her chubby cheek.

I go out to the hall and walk around the house. I am a restless soul, haunted by pain and suffering, shame and worry. I feel my heart beating so loudly, I am surprised the neighbour hasn't called to see if he can 'elp. My skin burns in the thawing, but in my bones I'm freezing. There is a cold in me that I think will never come out.

I look outside and see the sky is changing from black to blue. The sun is out there, stirring, ready to come over the Earth and then over the woods behind the house.

I go to the garage and open the door. I grab the weed and one-hitter and lighter from the garage stairs. I shut the door and leave it unlocked.

I unlock the front door as well.

I go to the fridge and grab a beer.

I leave the beer on the kitchen table and find a bathrobe. With the bathrobe over my arm and my hands full, I slide open the patio door. When I close it behind me, I leave it open an inch. The cat sticks his claw through the gap, grasping for freedom. I walk carefully to the hot tub, open it and step in.

I make a quick exclamation of pain, and a teardrop comes from my eyes.

I am through. I am on the other side of pain, and could get to the other side of any pain if I could endure what I had tonight. I am a king of kings. Lionized.

I relish this last moment of cold. I crack my beer, take a sip, place it in a cupholder and slide down into the tub until I am under water and the lion is soaked and lets go of my head. I feel like Sam McGee in the burning boat.

The Northern Lights have seen queer sights

But the queerest they ever did see

Was a fat naked man

(But with style and élan)

Who wished he had brought out his key.

The End

SCARED

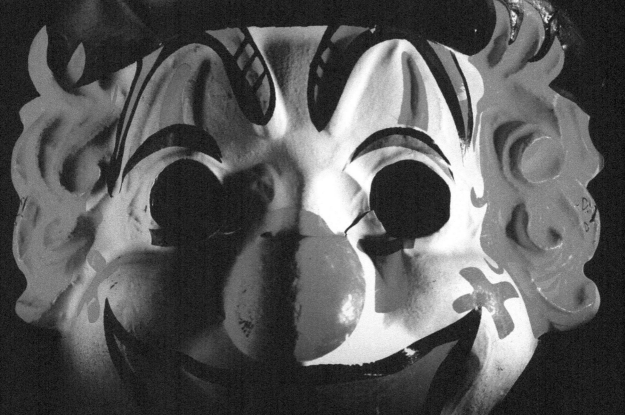

Scared

(album: Day for Night)

The client parked his car on a quiet street. It was a February night in an industrial part of Montreal near the Lachine canal. In the fogged light of the streetlamps, paper and trash circled in the wind, and there was a feeling of low pressure in the air. It seemed to kill all ambient noise, so that the report of a garbage can overturning in an alley came very sudden and sharp. In a heavy overcoat, the man walked up the block to a squat building. The building's only visible light, the only light on the block, shone out the window of the front door. The man entered a hallway, yellow paint peeling and mould in the corners, and walked up the stairs to the third floor.

The room number he looked for was etched on the frosted window of an office door and a light shone from inside. He opened the door, entering a small anteroom with a secretary's desk opposite him, and a small couch along a wall. The man was middle-aged, his thick brown hair graying in patches, his skin a heavy leather, folded and pinched around his mouth and eyes. He was tall and broad, with a barrel belly. He only stood alone in the room a moment before an inner door opened, and the client got his first look at the man he'd come to see.

"I'm Brandt," the client said, offering his meaty hand.

"Papineau," the second replied. "Welcome. Please, hang up your coat."

He indicated a closet in the anteroom, in which only a pale orange woman's coat hung. Brandt hung up his coat. He wore a brown suit of an expensive wool that dressed his large frame majestically.

"Come in, please, Mister Brandt," Papineau said, his hand leading Brandt's eyes into the dimly lit inner office. It was a room of polished wood, furnished in dark luxury.

"I'm sorry I'm late," Brandt said as he stepped across the threshold. "I came straight from the office, and I got lost."

Papineau glanced at the client's suit and shoes.

"I don't imagine you would come to this area often. I hope you did not feel unsafe," Papineau said. His accent was of Quebec City, clear and melodious, although he spoke slowly for a Quebecois.

Brandt walked by a large desk, as Papineau waved him into the chestnut leather chair in the middle of the room.

The host shut the door. Light came only from a brass desk lamp and barely reached the bookshelves lining three of the walls.

"A drink, Mister Brandt?"

There was a wheeled side-bar proffering a crystal decanter of amber liquid. Two glasses sat on the bar, the glass so pure they almost weren't there.

Papineau poured, and as Brandt took the glass in his hand, the drink seemed to give off a thin steam. Papineau placed his own glass on the desk and walked behind it. He was not old, though his sharply parted hair was more silver than black. He was a small man, in a pitch-black suit, with a white shirt and white silk tie. There was a slow smoothness in his movements that made Brandt think of a man in water.

Papineau removed a book from the shelf, and placed it before him as he sat down.

"Tell me, Mister Brandt," Papineau said in that French way, half intense, half joking, "Why did you make this appointment?"

"I heard about you. Not directly, but from someone at the office who knew someone. He said you scared the crap out of his friend. That you were like a carnival house of horrors for grown-ups."

"Why does that appeal to you?"

"I want to be thrilled."

"This is not a thrill ride, exactly. My office is not a roller-coaster where you scream and then walk away laughing on wobbly legs. The fear I sell reaches you right inside. Perhaps…"

"I need to feel something bad," Brandt interrupted. He was afraid of losing this already, before it had begun. "I have so much in my life that is good, and the feeling is not fulfilling to me. In fact, I think it's deadening. I think maybe I need to feel something powerfully bad to be able to feel anything again. To take away my complacency."

Brandt's left hand moved onto the desk. His wedding ring glinted in the light, next to a blue plastic toy ring, a cereal box prize. His hands were thick and utilitarian looking, and, while the skin showed purple lines of healed scarring, they were smooth.

"I want you to make me scared, Monsieur Papineau," he said, leaning forward.

"I can make you scared," Papineau said, "if you want me to. That's what you've paid me to do."

Papineau raised his glass with a smile, and Brandt leaned further to touch his to it with a musical clink. When Brandt kissed the glass to his lips he at once felt his anxiety of being here overcome. The room, the drink, the gentleness of Papineau's voice, all impressed Brandt as artefacts designed to bring comfort. To maintain in a client some feeling of a haven here, no matter what went on in their entertainment.

Papineau tapped on the silver cover of the book on his desk.

"This is my family bible," he said. "Tell me, Mister Brandt. Are you familiar with Ecclesiastes?"

Brandt had earlier taken off his tie and undone his collar, and he felt Papineau's stare on the little silver cross below his throat.

"No," he answered.

"It's quite beautiful. Written by King Solomon, of the mythical wisdom and wealth, son of the great conqueror, King David. Vanity of vanities, Solomon said. All is vanity."

Papineau's voice was smooth and nuanced as though it were of nature, of a kind with wind through a forest.

"Well. Here is what I propose to do," he continued. "I'll need to know just a little bit about you. If you're honest, I can make you scared. I'd like to commence by asking you to tell me a story of a time in your childhood that you were very afraid."

"Alright," Brandt said. "Maybe I'd better have a drink."

"Yes, Mister Brandt. Please do."

Brandt had thought about this story before coming in. Still he paused, sipped, and looked around the room. The liquor danced on his tongue. The weak light flickered on the trim of the ceiling like a wave, granting the impression of motion to the room, as if the trim itself were rotating.

Brandt spoke in a clear, assured voice. "When I was about nine, my family took me to New York for the Christmas holidays. For New Years, we went to Times Square. I remember being so excited to stay out after midnight. After they dropped the apple, we began to make our way back to the hotel slowly, as my dad was pointing at all the shops and lights. They got distracted looking in a store window, and I stepped away for a moment. I just wanted to feel what it was like there without my parents, pretending I was independent. Not an adult mind you, just independent. I wasn't paying attention."

"Go on, Mister Brandt."

"There were so many people towering over me, I was enclosed and had no sense that I'd moved, and I lost my parents. I tried to circle around, because I couldn't go against the crowd. Then I was in a side street and suddenly it was quiet and dark. Then I saw eyes. Eyes in the dark, peeking from alleys, hovering behind dumpsters. They were all looking right at me, or at least so I felt. I began to panic. I had this sense that if I turned around I'd be showing all the eyes that I was lost and afraid. That I was prey. I had a real sense that I had to keep going forward, or I'd be prey. Then some of the eyes came forward, and I saw men: bums and punks. It seemed like they were all around me, although there were only a few of them. I could see just twenty feet away the crowds on the next street. Then a man grabbed my arm. He asked if I had any change. I ran from him into the next street, and fought backwards through the crowd. It seemed impenetrable, like swimming upstream. I just started crying and kept pushing on. In those few seconds I felt like my old life was over, that I'd never find my parents again, and that I'd have to live and survive among those eyes in the dark. Then I heard my name, and I was in my mother's arms. I cried like an infant the whole walk home. I was humiliated."

There was quiet as he finished the story.

"And then you had the nightmares," Papineau said. "Of the eyes in the dark."

"Yes," Brandt said. "It became the only really irrational fear of my childhood."

"Do you have any irrational fears now?"

Brandt laughed. He had not allowed the memory to captivate him personally, yet it was still a relief to be through it.

"Yes," he said. He had thought about this topic as well. "I am always afraid of irrational things when I'm alone. If I swim in the ocean alone, I'm afraid of sharks. When I camp alone, I'm afraid of bears, or even axe murderers. It's as if I only believe that a horror story could happen to me when no one is watching; any witnesses make me immune."

"Well, I am here, so you shall not have any irrational fears," Papineau said. "I think that you have another fear. Your family - you believe that to be your weak spot. Am I correct?"

"In what way?" Brandt asked.

"The usual way, I suppose. You are not home as much as you should be; you work long hours. You are not as involved in their lives as you think you should be. You do not spend as much time with your wife. You are afraid of what kind of man this makes you. And worse, you think perhaps that it is because of your family that you are here, looking for something more interesting. Is this true?"

"Yes. I suppose you could say that."

"You wonder what are the implications for a man who is almost ready to admit to himself that he resents his family the time he spends with them, because he'd rather be working."

Brandt did not answer. This topic seemed a little off the track of what he expected, at least, the way Papineau raised it.

"These are unimportant issues," Papineau said. "A superficial fear, I believe. Because you recognize this problem, and you are an intelligent man, Mister Brandt, I see that. And you recognize this problem and maintain it, which tells me that you have reasons, reasons which you've weighed in your heart and chosen. Because you've worked hard, and you're proud of that. Because a man should achieve something in this life, or try to at least. What else, after all, is the purpose? And you make the money that keeps your family so comfortable, and affords them every opportunity and every security to do what they want with their lives. And that's an important gift, too, isn't it?"

"I think it is," Brandt said. "And I am proud of my work."

He supposed Papineau was measuring him out for something.

"Yes, I think we are barking up the wrong tree," Papineau said.

The host took a drink, then stood to refill Brandt.

"It's good isn't it?" Papineau said. "I discovered it in the Philippines and have it imported specially."

"It's excellent," Brandt said.

Papineau sat down.

"Still," he began, "obviously your family is important in your life. Tell me, is your wife Catholic?"

"Yes," Brandt said.

"And you raise your children Catholic, yes?"

Papineau smiled and tapped the silver plated book on his desk.

"Religion. You would laugh at the thought of risking your business on an out of date rumour. Yet."

He tapped the bible again.

"You bet everything, everything, on an ancient tale, full of contradictions. And imagine the consequence if you get any of it wrong, why, the penalty is eternal damnation and nightmarish suffering. That's what the book promises. Do you know your Testament well?"

"No. I don't remember too much."

Papineau looked at him quite seriously. "Horrific imagery, the afterlife as promised to those who worship wrong. Do you ever think of the grand cosmic battle, of angels, and anti-Christ, and pits of Hell promised by your old story?"

"No," Brandt said. "I really don't think of that at all."

He watched Papineau with a curiosity as to what would come out of the man's mouth next. It was confounding, and had turned altogether into something he had not expected.

"No, I don't suppose this matters much to you," Papineau continued. "For, should your own religion be true, then you would surely burn in Hell. Am I correct in this?"

Brandt breathed deeply and squirmed slightly in his chair. He lifted the glass to his lips to delay as he thought. He was conscious of some energy linking him to Papineau, making the outside world seem a distant dream.

"You are familiar enough with your religion to judge this, I am sure," Papineau said. "You know of mortal sins, you know of the Commandments."

This question, Brandt had not mulled over prior to the visit. His thoughts were following directions he would normally have cut off.

"Yes," Brandt said. "I suppose I would suffer were my religion correct."

"And your wife. She is very beautiful, but she also is not so religious."

"What of it Monsieur Papineau?"

"She is a passionate woman," Papineau replied. "She is temperamental."

"Where do you get all this?"

"You give away more than you know. And you have given your wife so much time to be angry with you. And she is not a strictly religious woman, to be sure."

"What are you getting at?"

"I am saying, Mister Brandt, that your wife has been adulterous. I am sure you have realized this yourself. In fact, you have factored this as a cost against the choice of work as your priority. Has this thought not crossed your mind? Remember that I asked for your honesty at the outset. Have you not thought this?"

"I have."

"And so you raise your children to believe in a religion that, should it prove correct, would consign both yourself and your wife to infinite torture and damnation. Mister Brandt, you should pray that your God does not exist."

Brandt regarded him with silent resentment. Papineau rose and turned to the bookshelf. He ran a finger along one shelf and looked at the spine of a volume he half pulled from its place.

Against the wall, the light hardly seemed to reach Papineau's face, his eyes disappearing in the shadow of their cavities, his white shirt collar alone reflecting brightly. He pulled the volume and cradled it in one hand as he flipped the pages.

"Do you suppose you are a good man, Mister Brandt? Is this what you think will ultimately save you, if there is a God, over any dogmatic code or Byzantine religion?"

"I suppose so."

"No, I did not take you for a strictly religious man. These tales of fire and brimstone will not frighten you when you leave my office. They will leave you as a ghost story dissipates in a child's mind at daybreak. I wonder what you do live for, Mr. Brandt."

Papineau sat back down.

"Are you familiar with the story of Faust?" Papineau said, indicating the book he placed next to the Bible.

"Sells his soul to the Devil."

"I am drawn to the aspects of Faust's loss of humanity. Enthralled with the powers granted by the Devil, Faust loses all interest in the mundane workings of our earthly world. I am compelled by this urge of man to find freedom in overthrowing his humanity. I wonder if there is something Faustian among the Nazi psychology."

Here Papineau paused, cocking his head as if a thought had occurred to him.

"I wonder why you consider yourself a good man, Mr. Brandt."

Brandt did not answer. Even as he had begun to dislike Papineau, the man's voice was hypnotic to the point that Brandt had to concentrate to understand his meaning, rather than just to feel it.

"Would you imagine," Papineau said, "that you would have risked your family and your life to harbour Jews in the Holocaust?"

"This is a rather childish question," Brandt said. "I suppose we'll never know."

"And I suppose there is no suffering in the world today that you could not help alleviate," Papineau said emphatically. "A good man, Mister Brandt? Because you've never killed anyone? Because you sit proudly as your business grows while elsewhere men starve, or are tortured to death? And while you have broken almost every other universally sacred commandment of religion? By what standards do you deem yourself good? There are a few here today who find ways to help those worst abused in the world. Just as there were a few in the Nazi territories. But you are not one of them here, where there is no real risk in such action, and you would certainly not have been one there.

"I don't think you worry much about goodness at all, Mr. Brandt. You concern yourself with your work. I do believe it would be no exaggeration to say that this is what you worship: it is what you devote yourself to and sacrifice for, it is what you find meaning in. What makes you so confident in the value of your work that you hold it above all other reasons for living?"

"What else is there?" Brandt said. "What else is there to be judged on other than what we can achieve? Great men do go down in history, Papineau. And they make that mark by dedication, and by belief in the value of their work."

"Ah, this I find quite funny, Mister Brandt. Tell me, how many names have come down to you from the whole of the Nineteenth Century? A handful of businessmen such as yourself. Rockefeller. Carnegie. A few dozen political or military leaders. Perhaps a few dozen more entertainers and artists. Out of hundreds of millions, mind you. But how many of those do you imagine will survive in the minds of the next generation? How many names remain from two thousand years ago? Are you the one in a billion who will be remembered beyond the death of your son's grandson? Don't you realize how short this memorial to your devotion will last? How useless your life has been, if this is what you've based it on, Mister Brandt."

Brandt pushed himself back from the desk and gazed at Papineau across the increased distance.

"How do you know what I think?" he asked.

"This is what I do," Papineau said. "Do you believe there is so much variety in men that I would not see in you what you have built your life on? Do you not know Mister Brandt, that there is no fear in a man's weaknesses, but only in his strength?"

Some physically instinctive reaction made Brandt take a large drink then, and he felt light-headed. Papineau opened his Bible to a marked page and began to read.

"'The words of the Preacher, the son of David, king in Jerusalem. Vanity of vanities, says the Preacher, vanity of vanities! All is vanity. What does man gain by all the toil at which he toils under the sun? A generation goes, and a generation comes, but the earth remains for ever.'"

Papineau paused to gauge Brandt's attention, then continued.

"'What has been is what will be, and what has been done is what will be done; and there is nothing new under the sun... There is no remembrance of former things, nor will there be any remembrance of later things yet to happen among those who come after. I the Preacher have been king over Israel in Jerusalem. And I applied my mind to seek and to search out by wisdom all that is done under heaven; it is an unhappy business that God has given to the sons of men to be busy with. I have seen everything that is done under the sun; and behold, all is vanity and a striving after wind... I said to myself, "I have acquired great wisdom, surpassing all who were over Jerusalem before me; and my mind has had great experience of wisdom and knowledge." And I applied my mind to know wisdom and to know madness and folly. I perceived that this also is but a striving after wind. For in much wisdom is much vexation, and he who increases knowledge increases sorrow.'"

Papineau looked up from the book and smiled. With his black and white clothes, his black and white hair, he seemed elemental, made from nature's first building blocks.

"Have I scared you yet?" he asked.

Still Brandt was quiet, and Papineau continued: "'Then I said to myself, "What befalls the fool will befall me also; why then have I been so very wise?" And I said to myself that this also is vanity. For of the wise man as of the fool there is no enduring remembrance, seeing that in the days to come all will have been long forgotten. How the wise man dies just like the fool!'"

Brandt's eyes were on the book as it shut. The Bible itself seemed to be insulting him. It was as if that passage had been tailored for his shape.

"You don't know what's inside me," Brandt said. "This is nothing but cold calculation. You know what buttons to push, like a carnival psychic."

"You are an intelligent man, you know the truth though you've hid from it so long. It has all been a lie, a construction to make you feel you've done something worthwhile in your life while all of it, all of it, is meaningless. Vanity."

Brandt was uncomfortable in his chair, and stood to refill his glass from the decanter. He could not prevent his mind from following all the implications of these ideas, filling in the spaces which Papineau's words left. In that space he was catching a glimpse of the entire history of man, there was a thread of meaning through it all, and he was grasping at that thread.

"You've debased all you valued as a child," Papineau said. "God, religion, respect of women, of relationships and honesty. Sacrifice for others. You have instead succeeded at hedonism and vanity. You see how your life has failed your childhood innocence. So you concoct more props to distract you until someday, you will die and hope beyond hope that this life is all there is."

"I don't want this thing between me and you," Brandt said. "I didn't expect a goddamn psychoanalysis, I expected a thrill."

"Yes, that's the deal!" Papineau said. "That I scare you. That's what you paid me to do. And perhaps the employee who sent you to me knew he was not doing the favour you believed."

Brandt felt the walls edging closer, inching in along the cherry-wood floors as Papineau stared at him, as Papineau now sipped from his glass without for one instant losing the probing intensity of his gaze.

"I imagine a man such as yourself has thought a great deal about greatness," Papineau said.

"I have, Monsieur Papineau."

"What made Alexander, Alexander? What made Caesar, Caesar?"

"Boldness," Brandt said.

"Cruelty," Papineau replied. "Savage cruelty. The seeking of greatness at all cost. Alexander was Alexander because he was merciless in subjugation, slaughtering whole populations, men, women and children. Alexander's greatness was incubated in blood. In a hundred years, or two hundred, Hitler and Stalin will take their place in the pantheon: as great conquerors first, as slaughterers second. Just as with those that come to us from the depths of history. Savagery is the surest route to greatness, but not the only. Greatness entails casting off one's humanity, whether in conflict through others… or through a single-minded devotion which overrides all human bonds. How can one build an empire while mindful of the human needs of kin or kindred souls? How can one immerse oneself in any enterprise while dealing with the mundane requirements of others? Greatness is cruelty in the service of vanity."

Brandt felt the floor disappear under him. His feet seemed to float in space, he felt the weightlessness flow up his body. Papineau's gaze was what held him there. If Papineau looked away, Brandt would tumble down into space, or Hell itself, which seemed surely now to wait below.

"Perhaps, Mister Brandt, the secret that Faust was handed was that greatness is found exactly in dismissing our humanity, that only in so doing could we become supermen. Perhaps this thought is what caused him such excitement. It was, after all, the Devil who presented that gift."

Brandt's face was colourless. The liquor in the invisible glass held in front of his face looked to Papineau's eyes as a splash of liquid bronze on a field of white ash.

"You make me scared," Brandt said. "It's what you do. It's not real."

He put the glass down on the desk in front of him, and his arm without it lost its power and fell to the armrest. His last words seemed to float away in the air, without the weight of their speaker's belief in them.

"Yes, you are scared," Papineau said. "Because we live in a world of which there are things to be scared. Because, existing in this world, we are capable of doing and believing scary things."

"If it is real… is there a way out?"

"Your children are your way out, Mister Brandt."

"My children?"

"You cannot define your life by your religion. You cannot define your life by your work or your virtue or your heroism. You can define your life by your family - because you, Mister Brandt, are only afraid when you are alone. I will not say this is God's gift. But it stands as the alternative to that gift which was given Faust."

"My children," Brandt said.

"And you should seize that gift, Mister Brandt, because you have so little time left to do so."

"What do you mean?"

"In one year, your oldest child will die."

The words now out of Papineau's mouth carried weight, like a gale wind that blew Brandt back into his seat.

"Why did you say that?" Brandt said.

"In one year, your oldest child will be killed by a reckless driver. By a man leaving my office."

"You're a liar!" Brandt leapt to his feet now, and found the floor underneath solid enough to support him. "How could you know that? It's you who are the Devil, Papineau! I should never have come here!"

Papineau's face now lost the humour it had held just below the surface for the duration of the interview.

"Please sit down, Mister Brandt."

"I will not sit down, Papineau. You tell me the meaning of what you've said."

"Very well," Papineau said. "It was a lie, a dart meant to extract sensation. Your children are safe tonight. Truth be told, they may live a long, long while. Only chance, not fate, holds their security."

Brandt exhaled slowly. His fists unclenched and he looked at Papineau with a passionless anger. He sat down again in his chair.

"It is funny how our lives rely on chance," Papineau said. "Look how the very meaning of your life now depends on the whims of daily security for your loved ones. How many lives can be crushed by one blow of chance? But this is the world we do live in, Mister Brandt. Your children, your life, depend on it like the air we breathe."

Brandt continued to breathe deeply and even that cold anger seemed to flow out of him with his breath, leaving him sagging like an emptied sack.

"Yes," Papineau continued, "they may live a long, long time, protected by whatever security your work has given them. But Mister Brandt, I ask you this one last question. What type of character do you suppose is shaped in children so smothered in that blanket of money you have thrown to comfort and protect them? You who have thought so much on the striving for greatness, the value of work. You who have considered the source of your own strength. Truly, what type of aimless, pointless future have you provided for your children by robbing them of any necessity to risk and work and achieve for themselves? What life of hedonism and nihilism do you see for them? All is vanity and a striving after wind - those were the words of Solomon the wealthy, son of David the conqueror. This is your hell, Mister Brandt. The unavoidable future you have given your children by your very quest for greatness. All is vanity."

Brandt sat very quietly now.

"I believe our interview is at its end, its unavoidable end," Papineau said.

Brandt stood robotically. The room, whose character had seemed so malleable, now returned to its former sturdiness around him.

"Remember, Mister Brandt, that there are many out there who understand Faust's secret. Many have not the material trappings of your life. And with Faust's secret, they do not fear to take. When you leave here, Mister Brandt, try not to be frightened by the eyes in the dark. It's been a pleasure doing business with you."

Brandt exited the office without another word, without looking at Papineau's face. He wrapped his heavy overcoat around him and left.

Outside, the car seemed so far down the street. He heard noises from the alleys, from the windows of the decrepit housing. He walked to the car without looking back.

The End

Little Bones

(Happy Hour Is

Here)

(album: Road Apples)

The thing is that if you have to wonder if you're cool, then you're probably not. So I used to wonder: how could people know they were cool? It was one of those philosophical questions with no answer, like the sound of one hand clapping, or the wood and the woodchuck. I sure never felt cool. I felt like I'd missed the starting gun. If I'd been there when they'd decided, I'm sure I could have made the cut, if I'd just known what they were looking for.

That summer, I was sixteen. The summer of the cottage party.

We'd been looking forward to it all week, all at our crappy summer McJobs. The cottage was a couple hours out of the 'Peg in Whiteshell. They were on a quiet part of a lake, no phone, no neighbours, so we wouldn't have to worry about anything.

Some guys were staying the whole weekend, but I was going up Saturday with Joel and Phil. And a 2-4 of Sleeman. Which was a lot for a sixteen-year-old, but there was all afternoon, and the next morning, and people always stole beers. I just didn't want to run out. There was nothing as hopeful as a cottage party.

We left before noon in Joel's dad's jeep, and it was blazing hot already. Phil and Joel, I knew, were cooler than me. Probably it would be better if I were on a team. Phil wasn't on a team, but he was a hippie. He got called on his cell from the cottage while we were still in town, and they said they had a motorboat and were skiing, and everyone had gotten completely loaded the night before. Awesome. Not to mention that Rebecca Lee, whose cottage it was, was a very hot girl. With hot friends.

Yellow prairies were out the car's back window; in front of us, the woods and the party. I remember that we listened to Sum 41 in the car, because I thought about the insane party from that music video and thought, fuck, that's so true.

The last part of the drive was a crazy dirt road for about two clicks. We had to park way down the driveway because there were already eight or nine cars there. We were each carrying a cooler, and our clothes, and a tent. I don't know why we each had our own tent. Actually, I do know, but it's not like we talked about it.

Actually, it's not like I'd even kissed a girl the last two years. Two years which, thank God, no one seemed to realize. Still, I always seemed to be just on the verge. I didn't consider it a statistically meaningful trend. It's just amazing how quickly years can go by.

When we got there, we waved at some guys on the back porch. Some others were down at the beach and the dock, and the boat was out on the lake, with someone skiing. Everyone was there, our whole group, and about three other cliques we were semi-attached to. That's what made a party in high school. When it was just your clique at someone's house, it was just a get-together. When your clique and others attached to it came, that made it a closed party. When cliques completely detached to yours came, that made it an open party, the kind that freshmen have that get their houses totally trashed. Of course, a get-together becomes a party if everyone gets hosed. This one at the cottage was a closed party, but a good one, with three separate cliques and some floaters. Rebecca Lee was in a semi-detached clique from mine. Well, I was kind of a floater too, really. Another strike against me in getting girls, because they're incestuous in the cliques. Although Joel was a bit of a floater too, and he definitely did better than me.

82

The cottage was my favourite kind: old wooden planks, surrounded by pine trees and Canadian Shield rock, which is igneous by the way. You know the three kinds of rock: Ignorant, Metaphoric and Sentimental.

My arms got rubbery from carrying a full cooler and stuff all the way up the driveway, and we all tossed our stuff inside. There were sleeping bags and backpacks and coolers all over, plus cases of empties on the wall. The furniture was all mismatched, with torn cushions, and the only decorations were a mounted fish and a framed picture of some old fuck on the wall. We cracked our first beers and went out through the screen door in back.

The patio caught the afternoon sun, Danny at the barbecue, everyone else around the patio table. Everyone was laughing and greeting us, and we were instantly in the party. Danny was not a guy I was crazy about. We'd had a good fistfight in grade nine. It was during a soccer game in gym class, but it was something that had been waiting to happen. Anyway, he was off-and-on an asshole, but he was friendly then. The rest on the patio were all buddies. A stereo was playing the Hip, Road Apples, which, as far as I'm concerned, is their party album. I mean, Day For Night? Great album, but you're not rocking on the beach to it.

There were five girls on the patio. Two had boyfriends, one other I knew I had no chance with, but two were theoretically possible, so therefore I spent a little time on the deck and had one of Danny's cheeseburgers, and the second beer was gone pretty fast. I was glad I brought a lot. I hadn't even got past the patio yet, which made it seem like there was plenty to do. It wasn't going to be the kind of boring party I can't stand, where everyone winds up playing dumb games or watching videos of people having fun at other parties.

Joel and I went down to the beach, a long stretch of grey, weedy sand. A bunch of the guys were playing football, and a couple girls as well, and a few other girls were sitting on towels. Two girls in bikinis, and one was Tina Tsong, who was an absolutely stunning Oriental girl with huge – just huge. Her bikini wasn't skimpy or anything, but holy shit! She never dressed too sexy at school, so the effect was huge. She got straight A's, so I'm sure she knew what she was doing to us.

I sat with her and her friend Terri, and they told me about waterskiing the day before, and how they'd gone out to a bridge that morning where some of the guys jumped off. They were drinking rum smoothies. Terri had scaly looking skin around her armpits, but her body was pretty good actually. Her hair was crinkly and greasy. She looked like she belonged in an arcade. She had this way of deferring to Tina and trying to act as her representative that I always found pretty funny. They were annoying to talk to for more than five minutes, actually. I was happy when a guy quit the football game and asked me to take his place, which is saying a lot considering Tina's bikini.

I took off my t-shirt and sandals to play. I was skinny, and a little awkward looking still, but I was pretty good at football, and I knew that I caught people by surprise. Sarah Morrison was there. She was a year older than most of us, and definitely one of the top four or five best looking girls going into grade twelve. She had wavy blonde hair, and wide tomboy hips, and her ass in those jean shorts was one of the best things I still to this day can think of.

It was five steamboat-rush. Our quarterback was Jimmy-P, a big Greek guy who was captain of the soccer team. He was good, but they had Scotty Mandatory at QB, and he was awesome. He was a sprinter, so whenever he couldn't find someone open, he'd just wait to be rushed and then sprint past the rusher and gain a bunch of yards. Scotty Mandatory was a nickname, meaning it was mandatory that he hit on every decent freshman girl. I'm pretty sure he got one of his friends to make up the name. I was also pretty sure he could've found more receivers open, but he definitely liked to hog it and run. He was showing off for Sarah, which, fair enough. I was covering one of the preppy kids who acted like he was a jock but really wasn't that athletic at all, so that was fun. After about half an hour, they were ahead, but we decided next touchdown wins.

Scotty Mandatory got them about twenty yards from the end zone, then screwed up a couple passes. On third down, my guy came straight down the left sideline at me, then broke diagonally across the middle. I gave him a step so that Scotty would think he was open. At five steamboats our rusher went in, but Scotty bombed it to my guy. I was right there. I jumped up and took it off my chest, into my hands. My snobby receiver was two steps past me before he could turn, and I had a clear sideline along the water's edge all the way to the end zone. I thought I did, until I heard people screaming and saw Scotty bearing down like a supersonic. I had to zig, which gained me a few steps, and that was enough for the touchdown.

I spiked the ball and ran in the lake screaming, "I'm going to Disney World!"

When the water was deep enough I dove in, and my team was still cheering. I felt so high I didn't want to come up and let it end, so I held my breath. I like stretching out fully underwater, and moving my body like a fish or Aquaman. I love being underwater. I knew I was drunk in the water.

Later, we were mostly on the patio and in the living room, and only a few guys were down to the beach or the dock. I was talking with the snobby receiver and another girl I knew, having a hot dog. Danny was at the barbecue again. I don't know why some people think they're in charge just because they're cooking the hot dogs. He also made chicken, and Sarah Morrison was eating a drumstick in her hands, and she had blackened sauce all over her fingers and lips. I was looking at her a lot, because she kept kind of obliviously licking her fingers, like, she was really into her chicken. She had no idea how great she looked. Then Danny says to her, "Baby, eat that chicken slow!"

I thought, What the fuck is that? How can someone say something so cheesy? And yet Sarah laughed right along with it, realizing she was making sexy-sucky face, blushing, wiping her lips. Even I felt like he almost looked cool saying it. I could never in a million years say that. I'd feel like an idiot. But it bothered me that such a dickhead could be cool to everyone. Wouldn't it?

The sun went down behind us. It sparkled at the far end of the lake, like it'd be a great day tomorrow. There was music blaring, and people were starting to do stupid shit. Fucking awesome.

Some guys started bringing wood down to the beach, and they got the fire going just as it got dark. Most of us moved down to the bonfire. I was talking to Rebecca Lee. Again, the snobby receiver was there. He was pretty damn funny though, so I enjoyed hanging out with him.

Sometime later, Phil and another friend of his pulled out the guitars. Normally, this would be the time I'd leave, but I liked Phil, and I even enjoyed his bonfire shit. Some songs they'd played together before, some they had to figure out. Phil sang some Bob Marley, Stompin' Tom, and GnR. Then he snuck in the Grateful

Dead, and Led Zeppelin, hippie stuff. Phil got a lot of chicks, and he always said it was his long hair. I always wondered about that.

Now that it was dark, shit was really getting funnier by the song.

Jimmy-P puked in the lake.

Barbecue Danny's girlfriend went off with a friend of his, and very soon everyone knew it.

Then two guys who were buddies got in a fistfight over Empiricism vs. Rationalism, which we'd been studying in history.

Then a dude pulled his bathing suit waistband open to show his buddy how loose it was, and his buddy stuck a flaming marshmallow in, and his pubes caught fire, and he ran into the lake right where Jimmy had puked.

I had another hot dog, cooking it on a stick in the fire. It tasted incredible, even though I'd dropped it in the ashes and I was pretty sure there was some of the stick broken inside of it. Rebecca left while I was eating, but anyways I didn't have a chance with her. I left snobby receiver and went to stand next to Tina. She was wearing clothes now, but I remembered. I tried to hit on her, but I got nowhere. Actually, I had no idea how people were even supposed to try, like, what one did to hit on one, but I tried for sure anyways. After she left, I realized that a lot of people had left the bonfire, including Phil, and just the other dude was playing now, singing Eagles songs. I went back up to the cottage.

The house was packed. The lights were off, and guys were dancing, and the whole place was shaking. There was a group out on the patio smoking, and the two guys who'd fought had made up and were doing shots off the picnic table, with their arms around each other's shoulders. I went right inside. I joined a circle in the middle of the floor and started dancing. I saw Tina walk out with a skater-dude I played tennis and studied algebra with. Fuck, I was a better tennis player than he was too! I was also better at algebra than him, but I knew that didn't get me anywhere, even with Tina who was the smartest girl in algebra herself. I danced with Terri, and we grinded a little bit, but then when I put my hands on her hips she pushed them away, and gave me the naughty-boy smiling headshake.

I was soaked with sweat and went out to piss with Joel. The two guys who were doing shots were still doing them, but you could see that they were angry again, and trying to hurt each other through Jagermeister. The sky was bright with stars. Joel and I tried to see who could piss further into the woods from the patio.

Joel said, "I feel like a king."

"It's regal and decadent here," I said. "I wish we could stay right here, right now, forever."

And I did wish it.

Gradually, the party came out on the patio as more and more people crashed inside. At some point, I tried to stage a comeback by turning the lights back on in the house.

Phil was in his sleeping bag, right by the door. He was smiling as I kicked him in the ribs half-hard, shouting, "Is it dead? Is it dead? Can it come out to play?"

"Nothing's dead down here. It's just a little tired."

You can never turn the clock back on a party.

I went back on the patio and started talking to Joel and Sarah. Joel ran track with her. They were talking about school this year, and I asked her where she was going to apply to university. She said she might not go right away, that she might take a year off and go out West. She was so hot. I got kind of into the conversation and asked her a bunch of questions and listened to stories about what she'd heard of Whistler liftie life, and working at the Banff Springs Hotel, and tree planting, and other things young guys did that sounded a hell of a lot more fun than anything I'd ever seen.

At some point Joel left and I just said fuck it, and asked her if she wanted to go down to the dock.

She said, "Sure."

I was flabbergasted, and worried that it showed in my face. But who recognizes flabbergast, eh? We walked down, still talking. I knew her parents were divorced, and I asked her if they both were okay with her taking a year off school. She just talked and talked, and she seemed glad to be talking, so I just shut up, which was just as well. She could really talk, and I felt like the more I said, the more likely I'd screw up. There were a lot of deer flies and mosquitoes distracting me, too. I was nervous, what with the two years since I kissed a girl, and this being Sarah Morrison, one of the top three best-looking girls in grade twelve. And she was cool, too. Not cool like image or attitude-wise, but cool, like, nice and smart. I nodded a lot. I was learning more about girls every second. We passed a few tents, and laughed at what was going on in a couple of them.

Things happened so quickly once we sat at the edge of the dock. Lake, stars, moons, and we were making out. Things were so good, and then they just got better. All kinds of great things were happening with our hands and legs. I had burst so fast beyond what I'd hoped for that it was all bonus now.

Then she went down on me.

I was wondering if there was anything I was supposed to do, other than enjoy myself. I just leaned back on my elbows. There was a massive deer fly on my thigh, but I couldn't do anything. Lake, stars, moons. It was funny because we had brought beers with us, and my mouth was so dry I was dying for a drink. But I thought it would look too cocky, so I didn't. She was amazing. This activity was amazing. Better than swimming underwater.

At the end, she spat off the dock and then rinsed her mouth out with beer and spat out again, and then guzzled the rest of the can. Shit, was I happy, although I remember thinking how the sinks in the house were lake water. We lay down beside each other. I didn't know whether or not to kiss her. But what the hell did I care, really, in proportion to everything? So we did.

She went back to the house when the sun woke her. My back was throbbing with pain from sleeping on the dock, but I pretended to be asleep because I could see she didn't want me walking back with her. I slept until my eyelids gave up against the sunlight, then jumped in the water. Aquaman.

When I went to the house, the guys smoking cigarettes on the porch made sarcastic comments about my bug bites, which I thought wasn't as funny as they thought until I went in and saw Sarah in the kitchen and the welts all over her face and arms. Which, maybe it's not right, but obviously made me happy. I wondered, when everyone thinks you've slept together, is it more respectful to say she just gave you a blowjob?

I kept my mouth shut. Sarah didn't talk to me, but she smiled when I looked at her. She wasn't making eye contact, but I knew she knew I was looking. I still had a few beers left. God, it never felt so good to open one.

The End

Looking For a Place To Happen

(album: Fully Completely)

The light of one candle flickered against the inside of the teepee's skin and wood ribs. Through the opening, an old priest stooped, and behind his dark shape the stars could be seen.

"Brûlé," the man in the door said. He went on in French: "Will you speak with me?"

On the furs in the warm belly of the teepee, the intertwined flesh moved. The white flesh emerged, sitting up while the brown-red body turned on an elbow and watched. From a pouch on the floor, the white man took some tobacco and placed it in his cheek. He stood, naked. He had a sheen of sweat, like a halo in the candlelight. Scars of varying ages and colours marked his lean body. Around his neck, a small wooden cross hung on a braided leather necklace. Brûlé felt at his crotch, then wrapped a loincloth and the pouch around his waist and stepped forward, ducking through the teepee opening as the old man backed away to let him out.

Brûlé 's was the only teepee within the village walls. In the dark night around them the sturdily built longhouses were quiet, but from the shaman's, perhaps four hundred feet away, a large fire was visible and the sound of men gathered could be heard.

Brûlé spit in the dirt at the hem of the old man's cassock.

"It is not a night for you, Curé Bernier," Brûlé said. "There are spirits in the air."

"There are new arrivals," the priest said. "But they are very much meat and bones. They come from the east. They bring stories."

"Stories or fairy tales?" Brûlé asked.

"That will be for our hosts to decide," Curé Bernier said.

The priests back was bowed, and his bony shoulders pointed up at his ears, but he walked with a sure step. His face was lined almost concentrically, like a mountain on a topographic map. It was hard to see where the skin ended and the white hair began, or any connection to the strong jawed young man who had crossed the ocean so many winters ago.

"Your hosts," Brûlé said. "I am no guest among them."

"We shall see what you are to them. The visitors say you sailed against Champlain, with the English. I wanted to warn you."

Brûlé was looking up at the stars, away from the village, over the trees. He seemed barely interested in the priest's conversation. Samuel de Champlain, the Father of New France, had brought Brûlé to this land as a boy servant. The two had been among the eight survivors of the Quebec colony from the bad winter of 1609. At just eighteen, Champlain had given Brûlé to the Hurons, as a kind of cultural ambassador. A chief's son was taken back to Paris in his place. Brûlé's adventures had been the greater. Twenty-five years Brûlé had been in this wild land.

Curé Bernier had been among the survivors of 1609 too. The priest had known Brûlé since his adolescence. Since that time, their paths had crossed every six or eight years. Brûlé always appeared at challenging times, and his appearance always added to the challenge.

"To warn me or to gloat?" Brûlé said finally.

"Perhaps to give you a chance to repent," Curé Bernier said. "You've wasted your life, Brûlé, but your soul can still be saved."

He was angered at how little his words touched Brûlé.

"That is my only business!" he added, his face trembling.

He wondered why he was angered: at the sin of a life Brûlé had led; or that he had the power to lead Brûlé to God nonetheless – and the obligation not to withhold that service; or that Brûlé did not care of any of it.

Brûlé began walking towards the edge of the pine forest, and the priest fell in step next to him. "Save my soul," Brûlé said.

"You still have the smell of that savage woman on you," Curé Bernier said.

Brûlé laughed. "I want my life to smell like this, Père. Of a woman of some ancient race, of an animal opened up to read the future in it, of a village of birch wood longhouses aflame. This is not that old place, don't you understand? Most of your life has been lived here, and you still do not know anything. Your god is out of his jurisdiction. Here there are ghosts in the trees; I've seen them. Your god and his laws served me little here."

He paused, recollecting with another laugh. His tone changed, like he was exchanging stories with an old friend: "When the Algonquin tortured me, I was wearing a cross. I invoked the god of the cross to threaten them, and then - lightning rent the sky. It was hours later, but it made a strong impression. They all regarded me with fear then, and let me free. Only in my lies did that cross serve me any value," he turned suddenly to the priest and winked. "I suppose the same could be said for you.

"You've traveled far in this New World, Père, telling your fairy tales. But there are tribes you'll never see. In many villages, I am the only white man they've known. A wasted life? You're a fool. I'll live in their legends forever. I've become a part of this land, and my name will last here longer than your fairy tales. And the white men who come here, too, will know my name, for they'll know it is behind me they have come."

"Your capacity for sin is matched only by your conceit."

"I've gone further than Champlain. He is still a European, a stranger in a strange land. I am the real explorer, because I've taken this land into me. I am the conqueror."

"It is of no advantage to your soul," the priest said. "You have discovered a place for your short, shameful life, and lost an eternity in heaven."

"Your heaven does not cover this continent," Brûlé said. "But if there is any such a thing as immortality, there will be a table for the explorers. And I'll have a seat equal to anyone's. Jacques Cartier, right this way. Monsieur Brûlé, come in, sit down, there's Erik the Red, at your left, and Marco Polo, Pizarro, Cortes. They have been expecting you!"

"Pizarro and Cortes led armies," the priest said. "They conquered empires for country and the cross. They brought civilization, while you've merely disappeared into the savages, and for nothing but yourself."

"Why should I conquer for some dead nation back across the ocean? This is a new world, and I've conquered it for myself. I've led Frenchman and English, Huron and Iroquois, in battle, and against all those too. But I've less blood on my hands than those Christian conquerors. Brought civilization? They brought slaughter and were despised. That is how they represented your god. I've seen further than any of those. And deeper. I have discovered lands of dreamlike beauty and bounty. I've hunted monsters. Seen spirits conjured by magic men. Mine is the life puny men in France wish for. In this astounding land, I go as I wish; welcome in all places. I follow every whim."

Brûlé stopped at a place where the moonlight came through the trees. He stooped to the ground and began gathering branches. He pulled something from his pouch, and a fire was started before the priest knew what Brûlé was doing. Brûlé sat on his haunches; the priest stayed standing behind him.

The young man spoke quietly over the crackling fire.

"On the mighty Ottawa I sacrificed tobacco to the spirit of the white water, and smoked their strange plants, and was driven to a frenzy as we danced in the great waterfall. That's when I felt holy, and it was the pagan gods or devils I felt touched by, not yours."

"Gods or devils indeed, it is not clear which these savages pray to."

Brûlé spat.

"Nor you, Curé Bernier," he said.

Now he pulled a knife with a stone blade from his loincloth and began cutting into a small branch. "I've learned their arts. Their spirits haunt me."

"They'll kill me, these people," Brûlé continued. "Because I shouldn't know these things. I've seen my destiny. So your news is no surprise, only a piece of the puzzle."

"This is where you will die then. Cursed by God."

Brûlé ignored him, concentrating on working the piece of wood in his hands.

"We all live hoping for a time and place in which to be great," he said without looking up. The skin was off the branch he was carving and it was creamy and shiny with sap in the firelight. "A shame to leave this masterpiece."

He was absolutely concentrated on that wood and that knife in his hands, yet the movement of the hands was smooth and natural.

"But I'll match it in death," he said. "I'll paint the scene in my mind from foreseen memories, just to know who murdered me. Then it will be my ghost in these trees."

The priest saw that the branch in Brûlé's hand had taken the form of a man, and as soon as he'd seen it, Brûlé tossed the figure into his small fire. The fire rose with a quiet surge, then went down again.

The End

Grace, Too

(album: Day for Night)

The rain fell in fat drops so that they were wet right away.
He tipped his fedora, and water poured off it. She laughed.

The End

The Darkest One

(album: In Violet Light)

When everything was falling apart, Simon and Dino met up for beers at a bar in Dartmouth.

They weren't old friends, but good friends; they had quickly found sympathy and understanding with each other, as though they'd been friends in another life. When Simon first arrived in Halifax, Cowboy had introduced him around. Dino was one of Cowboy's new Halifax friends; Simon was one of Cowboy's old Toronto gang.

Simon liked Dino because he was simple. No, he liked him because he was a nice guy who laughed at his jokes, but he liked him especially because he was simple. Not in the sense of dumb at all; rather, straightforward and open. Everyone Simon knew, especially back home in Toronto, all their attitudes and everything they said seemed faked, contrived based on some intellectual calculations. Dino seemed immune to that. He was one of those people who simply thought what he thought. The complexities and layers of truth, which clogged so many minds, were foreign to him. That instinctiveness made him seem to Simon both clean and real.

Dino was a mechanic, and soon phone-instructed Simon through several do-it-yourself engine overhauls. With each, Simon became more in Dino's debt, a debt the young mechanic always denied existed. That was the situation from Simon's point of view when, for Dino, things went wrong.

Dino's partner in the garage, a Kenyan immigrant, left first. Perhaps his senses were acute to the smell of impending disaster. One day, he just disappeared.

The partner had always been the one to wring money from their deadbeat customers; Dino was too nice to chase and threaten. The money problems began quickly.

Then Dino's wife left, taking their baby son.

With his partner gone, there was no time to breathe it in; Dino was at the garage twelve, sometimes fourteen hours a day. His wife was asking for child support money, threatening him through the access to his child.

Dino was shy and passive. He was one of those who took what life gave him - the law was an opaque force to him. He lacked that instinct for knowing when an individual might fight fate. The idea that he might have certain legal rights of his own would not occur to him. For weeks he worked those long hours, as his home fell into disrepair. Feelings of great frustration and sadness occasionally flitted across the screen of his conscious mind, that otherwise concentrated on leaking gaskets, corroded wires, alternators, timing belts, transmissions, water pumps, and body work. He would go days of sweaty, oily work without washing, sleeping in his clothes, even sleeping in the garage.

The electric car-lift in the garage broke, and Dino didn't have the money to repair it. Without the lift, all his repairs took longer, but Dino never charged more than the book value for a job, so that he might work three or four hours on something and charge the two hours listed as standard in the book. His debts piled up. For the first time in his life he felt depression, an irresistible inertia; a dampening that seemed to make movement, even thought, exhausting. He went to work less and less, refusing new jobs. Then he stopped going in at all, and soon the garage was abandoned, the junk cars in the yard left for the property owners to scavenge. It was the collapse of a life.

Simon took Dino for beers that night hoping to cheer him up, or somehow motivate him for some new endeavor, to take another crack at life. At least, to distract him for a few hours. Over beers, baby-faced Dino mused about joining the French Foreign Legion. As crazy as it was, it excited Simon to hear. It was wilful action, and wilful action was what Dino needed. It was the kind of action Simon could dream about but never pour his own flesh-and-blood life into. It was exotic to Simon, and he wanted someone he knew to do something like that.

Simon encouraged Dino in his Foreign Legion fantasy; mired in his depression, Dino seemed intoxicated in breathing life to his thoughts. More beers came, empty mugs taken.

"Do you ever fantasize," Dino said, looking right into Simon's eyes, "about everything just falling apart? I wish there was a do-over for the whole world, with just chaos and total violence, and it was every man for himself. A clean slate. All you had to do was survive. I don't know if the Russian Revolution was like that, but that's what I imagine. I'd like to live through that kind of thing."

Simon remembered that remark because Dino was the most good-natured, gentle man he knew. He knew Dino must be in a bad place with his situation, but had never imagined his dark thoughts could be focused externally. Simon thought, this is the sound of a frustrated man, and he felt sorry for him, even as Dino became giddy continuing the confession of his fantasy.

Dino backed out on the Foreign Legion idea eventually, when he realized that the five-year commitment would mean five years without seeing his son. Instead, he joined the Canadian army. Cowboy ridiculed it at the time. Simon thought it would be good for him: a distraction, some discipline, a steady paycheque to support his kid. On top, it seemed so unlike the quiet, conservative-living Dino that the idea itself was entertaining.

Cowboy had known Dino a long time before Simon had come to Halifax. Simon thought Cowboy patronized Dino; condescended to him. Simon saw something in Dino, a strange potential he imagined Cowboy did not see. When Dino spoke of the Foreign Legion, and then the Canadian Forces, Cowboy would tell Simon, half-jokingly and in front of their friends, to quit encouraging Dino in his weird fantasies.

But Dino loved the army. He was a natural athlete, tough and focused, and he excelled at the various skills that make up a modern soldier. He loved being able to concentrate without having to think. Being an officer or NCO was no ambition for him. They didn't pay him enough to think, only to march and shoot. He was with 2nd Battalion, RCR in New Brunswick. It was a mechanized infantry unit. With Dino's background, he could easily have avoided the dirty work by specializing as a technician. But he was done with mechanics, and preferred the life of a grunt.

Sleeping in cold muddy ditches was not a drawback of the job to Dino, it was an attraction, he confessed to the two friends, responding to teasing by Cowboy about the discomforts of his career. Simon considered himself fairly tough: he played rugby and had been in more barroom fights than he could count. He found himself jealous of the physicality and roughness of Dino's new life. Simon was a weekend camper, while Dino came indoors only on his weekends in the city, it seemed.

Dino never lost his good nature, and what seemed more amazing to Simon and Cowboy, he had friends in the army. His mind itself was opening through all the varied soldiers he was spending time with. He became for the first time aware of the world of abstract thought, at the same time as being exposed to the very real points-of-views and ways of life he'd never personally experienced. It was like a tear in the cocoon that had always sheltered his mind. Cracks were forming quickly.

Dino's thoughts were like a house-pet that, after many years indoors, is suddenly allowed out and sees open spaces and high skies for the first time.

On the weekends when he came home, Simon and Cowboy's continuing project was simply to get Dino laid. Dino was uncomfortable with strangers, and even with his baby face he would frighten women away when he'd quickly start going on about whatever area of metaphysics he'd lately been thinking about.

He had a suddenly voracious appetite for ideas and discussion. He'd never finished high school let alone gone to university where he might have bored himself out of this kind of late night dorm-talk long ago. He was open to a lot of things he'd hear from guys in his unit. Much of it was bullshit - re-formulated hippie pseudo-religious trash, or conspiracy theories. Simon warned Dino not to be gullible, to develop the old bullshit-detector.

Dino was not too proud to admit he needed help, or to admit inferiority on some ground. He asked Simon for guidance, books that could really show him what was what. This was how he approached philosophy, literature, religion, world history, political science. He imagined Simon had read the library and had personally worked out a formula synthesizing and measuring it all. Simon was at a loss how to direct him. But he promised to look into things and work out some recommendations.

The time came when the 2ⁿᵈ Battalion was sent to Afghanistan. A six-month tour.

When 2ⁿᵈ Battalion came back, Simon and Cowboy were at pretty much the same places in their lives. Dino seemed different.

The first time Simon saw him, he was all jet-lagged and drunk and didn't make much sense. But after that, when they were helping Cowboy move apartments, Simon really saw the change. Dino was more confident; he seemed personally more powerful. He was physically strong and fit. He'd applied for the elite forces and felt he had a good chance at making the selection. This was what the army was supposed to do for him, and it made Simon happy. He felt as though he'd won a silent argument with Cowboy. But something worried him. Perhaps his own sense of superiority was jarred by the new confidence of his friend.

There were other changes. After joining the army, Dino had taken up meditation. Now he had mantras tattooed on his hands, and a great many ideas on spirituality. In Afghanistan, when he wasn't on patrol, he'd spend his time meditating in the hills around Kabul. It had been a peaceful posting. Dino came home only a week before the Canadians started getting hit by Taliban insurgents in Kandahar.

On Cowboy's balcony, sharing a beer break from the moving, Dino talked about the "welcome back" from his parents.

"My grandfather fought in two world wars for Italy," Dino said. "When I came home, my dad cried."

116

"Was your grandfather a mountain man like your dad?" Cowboy asked.

"Oh, yeah. They were backcountry from north Italy."

"Did he fight for Mussolini then?" Simon asked.

"Well, I don't know which sides there were," Dino said.

"There were the fascists," Simon said, "with Mussolini, and then… Italy switched sides at the end, actually."

Dino began remembering things he'd heard in his family.

"Italy was in a tough position," he said. "Mussolini is not just what we hear. History isn't always complete, especially when you lose. He raised literacy. He built a lot of infrastructure in Africa. He fought the mafia."

"Yeah, Mussolini made the trains run on time," Simon said. "That's the classic defense of fascism."

"But was he really fascist or is that just what people say?" Dino said.

He was questioning things in such a way that seemed almost charming. He asked such big questions from such holes of ignorance that he had no concept of the question's bigness. Simon wondered how someone this curious wouldn't know the sides in World War II, when his own grandfather had been in the war.

"No, no," Simon said, "He was pretty much the definition of fascism. That was his philosophy."

"Was he also involved with the bad stuff, with Hitler?" Dino asked.

"Yeah," Simon said. "He was involved with the bad stuff. But he made the trains run on time."

Dino nodded, as if ingesting. He moved his eyes away, looking around the room.

"I think things are going to get bad soon," Dino said, trying to steer the conversation to the ground he wanted to explore. "I think we're living in fucked-up times."

Sometimes you could see he'd been thinking about something while he was away and wanted to try it out on Simon. He'd been away a long time, this time.

"Let's go," Cowboy said, seeing it coming and not at all interested. "We've got to go to the old apartment and throw out garbage bags."

They walked down fifty-seven stairs to the car parked beside the snow bank.

"Where do you think the major fuck ups are coming from?" Simon asked.

"I don't know," Dino said. "Everywhere. We can't stop bad countries from doing bad things the way things are; it's a joke. The UN does nothing in Rwanda, in places where there's genocide. Because it all involves politics. I just see how amazingly efficient the army is: we have a problem, we make a plan, we carry out the plan… It makes the UN and all the stuff the army *doesn't* deal with seem pathetic.

"They need to change the system so that there's more clear-cut action based on facts. The UN needs a standing army. Now it takes so long to gather any forces, and countries only volunteer for *some* missions. If they had a standing army the UN wouldn't need to be tied to bullshit national politics. They could just act on what needs to be done."

"Jesus," Simon said as he slid into the driver's seat, Dino into the passenger's seat, Cowboy crowding into the back among the skis and hockey gear. "So your solution to a dysfunctional UN is to give them more power and a standing army?"

"Turn left at that alley," Cowboy said. "You can cut right through there to my old street."

"I'm saying that we need to take the decision-making out of it by making clear-cut criteria and looking at clear-cut proof of humanitarian abuses and things like that," Dino said.

"So, when your UN police force invades China for torturing or executing political prisoners, how's that gonna' go over, world-peace-wise?"

"No, well, obviously it wouldn't be just about force. There would have to be concessions to maintain world stability."

"Sounds a little like what we've got," Simon said.

They parked and walked up to the second floor apartment. Garbage was strewn around the room: plastic bags, soda bottles, broken furniture. Cowboy carried full garbage bags down to the curb, while Simon and Dino set to tossing the old furniture off the balcony.

"What we need is the ability to respond quickly and decisively to humanitarian problems," Dino continued. "If we had a constitution so that the triggers and conditions were clear. I mean, it should be very clear that you can't teach kids to hate and kill -"

"So now we're running all the world's education systems too?"

"No, we're not forcing anything on anyone, we just need experts, not politicians, charismatic leaders who can express what needs doing."

They argued further, with Simon wondering where Dino had been getting these ideas.

At some points, Simon would get annoyed at Dino's naïveté. He'd mock him, as the quickest way to quiet him, but Dino didn't seem much phased by the mocking anymore.

Cowboy diverted them finally, saying, "Dino, you've been in the army over a year now, aren't you ready to fucking coup this place?"

"What, Canada?" Dino asked, before realizing Cowboy was joking.

They laughed.

"Do you learn anything about throwing coups in the army?" Simon asked. "How insurrections happen?"

"No," Dino said. "But… how would you take over Canada if you were in that business?"

Simon thought for a moment.

"I don't know," he said. "I think with people like Lenin and Hitler, they had an army of the total bottom dwellers of society. Angry people with nothing to lose. There's just not enough of a base of total losers in Canada that would want to throw a monkey wrench in things."

When they got back to the car, before they stepped in, Simon stopped and turned.

"Dino, I'm just kind of curious, from the words you were using and some of the things you were saying… Have you been reading Mussolini or Hitler's writings?"

"No, no I haven't."

"I have an idea," Simon said. "Let's play a game. Let's figure out how we would coup Canada. We'll read all about this stuff. I'll send you some things to read, we'll both do research, and talk plans - propaganda, our base of support in the population, military components, organization, whatever is involved. I'll download Hitler's Mein Kampf and Marx's Communist Manifesto to start, and then I'll forward them to you."

"Yeah, well, let's do what you say. Send me an email and we'll go back and forth. I like this," Dino said. "I've had this discussion with a lot of people and your arguments against me are the best I've heard yet."

That's how the game started - the game Simon had been looking for his whole life. Simon sent Dino Fanon's *The Wretched of the Earth*; Camus' *The Rebel*. Simon was very interested in the psychology of the rebel. What made him tick. Dino loved it all, and Simon loved the questions he'd ask. They'd talk intensely from the couches in Cowboy's living room, talking right past Cowboy - how to build a serious movement, what instincts to appeal to. Cowboy, in turn, chided Simon for playing with Dino like a toy, which Dino took with a laugh. You'll break him, Cowboy warned. His brain's gonna' explode. Then, Simon would talk about Cowboy as if he weren't there, telling Dino that Cowboy was jealous because he never though about anything more interesting than Liverpool and the Premiership.

It was a winter of intellect. Dino surprised Simon by sending him Caesar's history of the Gallic Wars, Napoleon's memoirs, and Sun-Tzu's *Art of War*. Between them they covered Mao, Lenin, Spartacus, Washington, the Ayatollahs, Che, and Riel. The few times they went out, discussing Rousseau and de Tocqueville over beers, Simon would introduce Dino to women, good-looking women who ate Dino up, especially once Simon told them he was just back from Afghanistan. Still Dino frightened them away, quickly turning from heroic to crazed and possibly dangerous with his relentless, passionate talk.

In the spring, Simon wanted to understand mind control, so they read about North Korea and Rwanda. Dino was interested in dictators that maintained popular support, so they read about Khadaffi and Milosevic.

In early summer, Simon and Dino went out for beers in Dartmouth, the same bar Dino had fantasized about the world falling apart, before the army.

"What do you think of Nietzsche?" Dino asked before the beers even arrived at the table.

Simon laughed. "Who turned you on to Nietzsche?"

"A guy from my unit. Have you read him?"

"Yeah. Great stuff," Simon said.

"You know what I like? How he talks about how our whole value systems are upside down. How we've let the worst parts of us dictate how we live. It makes you really think about everything, not just how you live, but how you live because of how other people live."

"Be careful, Dino," Simon said. "Nietzsche is to be talked about, not lived."

"Well, I guess that's the difference between you and me. I say what I mean, and I mean what I mean. This country's so politically correct that most people don't."

"What do *you* have to say that's so politically incorrect?" Simon said. He was stung by Dino's comment and wanted to put him in his place.

"Never mind," Dino said.

They moved on to other things: hockey and army life and Simon's job at the marketing firm. When they left, they said goodbye in the warm bar, as Simon went straight out while Dino went to the bathroom.

The bar was in a bad area. Late on a weeknight, there was no one in the streets. Walking to his car alone, Simon heard a voice call to him. He turned to look in the shadow behind a building, and a man flashed a knife towards his chin, grabbed him by the collar and pulled him into his alley.

He had the eyes of a junkie, but his hand was steady with that knife.

Simon began pulling the wallet from his pocket, trying not to take his eyes off the mugger's. He didn't see Dino seeing them.

With the force of a bus, Dino rammed the mugger, the two bodies flying away from Simon with a crash into the garbage cans and onto the ground. Simon saw Dino's elbow piston back for three quick punches, then he rose, pulling the junkie up, and flung him forward. The junkie regained his balance and continued running the hell away.

"Holy fuck, Dino, thanks," Simon said.

Dino looked at him funny. He leaned into him quickly, with a forearm across Simon's throat, forcing Simon back against the wall. Simon was helpless with Dino's weight on his chest, and very suddenly afraid again.

"You see what a fucking upside down place this is?" Dino said. "People like you can't even protect yourself without people like me to take care of you. Yet people like you make twice as much money and get twice as many women."

Dino let go of Simon and walked away. Simon nearly collapsed. He had felt weak during the entire encounter; afterwards he felt as though he didn't have a body at all.

They didn't speak in the days that followed.

Weeks later, Cowboy called Simon. Dino had been deployed to Haiti, Cowboy said, a UN police action. He was off for four months.

"He's got my speakers," Cowboy said. "You still have a spare key?"

"Sure," Simon said, and when Cowboy came by, Simon decided to join him on the errand.

Dino's place was also in Dartmouth, a one-floor apartment in a run-down townhouse in a neighbourhood of run-down townhouses. The neighbour's cat was on the wooden front porch.

The lights were off inside, and the switch didn't correct it.

"I'll find a flashlight," Cowboy said, stumbling down the hall to the kitchen.

Simon heard him fumbling through cupboards, and then saw the cone of light of a flashlight, dust hanging thickly in it.

Cowboy walked back through the hall and flashed the light into the living room.

The first thing they saw was a wall-sized topographical map of Haiti, covered in scribble.

Turning the flashlight around the room, they saw the walls covered in pages torn from books, the pages covered in scribbles, with passages highlighted and circled.

On the floor were the torn-out book covers, discarded like chicken bones.

124

There was Marx, Mussolini, Mao, Machiavelli and all the other books of their study group, mixed with books on Haiti, on its history of violence and overlords, on its people, on its spirituality, and its geography.

Cowboy did a slow pass along one wall as they walked towards it close enough to read aloud the highlighted fragments on the pages:

"In no case have great movements been set afoot by the syrupy effusions of aesthetic litterateurs and drawing-room heroes -"

"Do you feel that Providence has called you to proclaim the Truth to the world? If so, then go and do it."

"The world itself is the will to power - and nothing else! And you yourself are the will to power - and nothing else!"

"I teach you the overman. Man is something that shall be overcome. What have you done to overcome him? All beings so far have created something beyond themselves; and do you want to be the ebb of this great flood and even go back to the beasts rather than overcome man? What is the ape to man? A laughingstock or a painful embarrassment. And man shall be just that for the overman: a laughingstock or a painful embarrassment"

"Laughingstock," Cowboy repeated.

The image of them each mocking Dino on Cowboy's couch flashed in Simon's mind.

"I guess he won't be needing the speakers," Cowboy said.

Simon looked at that map a long time, even after Cowboy turned the flashlight beam away from it.

The End

Put it Off

(album: Trouble at the Henhouse)

Dear Amber,

This is your father. There, that's over with. So now either this letter is in the garbage, or you've sat down or taken a breath or whatever and kept reading. I'm sorry for your loss. I'm not trying to swoop in and be your dad. I'll say my piece and you can choose if you want me in your life.

Your mom was a beautiful person. I know this feels right now like a sadness that will never go away. And maybe it never will, but I know your grandparents love you and will take care of you, and I know, if you're Jen's daughter, that you're strong and you'll kick ass whatever scars you have.

I've wanted to write you every day of your life. I couldn't. Every time I'd start, I imagined your mom throwing it out, or worse, opening old scars. I didn't know what your mom told you and I didn't want to confuse whatever story you had. Each day that I didn't write made it harder the next day. I knew you didn't need me. Maybe now, there's a chance you maybe do. That you could use someone. I don't want to say a dad. I don't deserve that name. But I could be someone to you if you want.

I knew your mom well. I'm just sorry for your loss. I don't really know what I can say to make you feel better, but I guess eventually you'll want to hear about me. And your mom, and you. Maybe you don't, but I don't feel like I can just say Sorry, Bye.

I don't know what your mom ever told you. I'll tell you what I can.

I'm a loser. If I'm being honest with you, I'm a loser. I never said this before. I always was a loser. I'm 37. I live in Edmonton. I work for an oil company, in one of the big ugly offices downtown. I have a brother. I play guitar. I met your mom at UBC.

We were in our last year. I was in fine arts. Visual arts. I flunked out, but she finished. We went out all school year, from September to April, then we just kept going. I don't think either of us saw ourselves together after April, but then it was May, and we were still together. Nothing magic happened between April and May. So we got our first jobs in Vancouver, and moved in together. I even met your grandparents. We were in Kitsilano. It was different then. We could afford a place. It was a pretty crappy place, especially to Jen. Your mom, your grandparents had a lot of money. They were from Montreal and your mom grew up in an old mansion in Westmount. We had a basement apartment in Kits and it stank from cat piss upstairs. But it was exciting and romantic. Maybe because it was so crappy and we were in it together. We both wanted excitement and romance, then.

Your mom was so special. She was beautiful and smart and ambitious. But I was selfish. I was a loser. I was into drugs and partying, and I lost my job as a security guard.

I don't know if your mom ever loved me. Maybe she liked my ambition at first. We were both big dreamers. She went into home sales. I don't know if she was still doing that, but she was great because everyone trusted her. I was gonna be an artist. I was gonna be an artist businessman, like, I would bring all my artist friends on my coattails and lead a movement. Like Andy Warhol. (Google him.)

I'm sorry, this isn't a beautiful story. She didn't love me enough, and I didn't love her enough, and she deserved someone who did. I knew she deserved better. I always knew, but I couldn't leave her either. You know your mom. She was a dreamer, but she was so real, and I felt so fake around her. I felt automatically like a worse level of human. It wasn't anybody's fault, it was just the way. She was so real, and happy, that I didn't have the guts to hurt her. It went on like that a long time. I think it was like that from the start.

Then your grandparents got involved. They cut your mom off. She should have listened to them and left me, but it made her more stubborn. Then, how could I leave her after she chose me over her parents? Don't blame your grandparents - they were right. I'm not like that now, but I was a user then. Maybe they didn't know that, but they knew I was going down and I was going to bring her with me. This was all before you came along.

***

He thought of all the times he'd tried to leave her. From the first month. The elaborate planning that went into it - weeks of set up, carefully putting ideas into her mind so that his reasons would make sense - so she wouldn't hate him for it. How he'd get drunk to get the courage, but he could never get that drunk. He thought how she was an addiction. He wondered, not for the first time, if she were the reason he'd drank and used, to avoid the problem. Then he felt shame for blaming her, that his addictions were his responsibility and no one else's, and what an asshole he was to blame a dead woman who couldn't defend herself for his weakness.

He'd thought this, too, before: that it wasn't fear for her feelings, but for his own loss of that safe shelter of strength and happiness. What had been the matter with him that he couldn't love her? He remembered how he would feel guilty after sex. Like he had fouled something pure. He was a degenerate, even if it was only in his mind.

She was religious, or had been once, but that wasn't where her vibe of purity and innocence came from. That was all her.

He'd wanted to be an artist. He really believed he needed to suffer; he believed he needed those drug fever visions. That this would make his art. Bigger, it would make his credibility. That people would believe he was an artist, so they would believe what he made was art. He really believed that, then. When he tried to make things, he would destroy them before anyone could see - except Jen of course. It was all just part of the process. He was going in the right direction. How had he ever been so dumb?

His friends became her friends - without her parents, she drifted towards his part of the world, of the city. But then he got new friends. People more fucked up than him. Maybe it was just to be apart, or to piss her off so she'd leave him, finally, where he belonged.

They never talked about abortion, though he thought about it non-stop in the first months. His two step-plan. It was maybe two years after he'd run away that he got it that this was a real person, a real girl, and he stopped wishing she'd never been born and began wishing her well. Maybe something good could come from him.

***

I knew that I would fuck up your life. That's the bottom line. I was using a lot then and my brain wasn't worth much, but I was smart enough to get that. I knew your grandparents would come back if I left, and they would be better for you, and

134

you and your mom would have money. It wasn't the money - I just knew that your mom and her parents were a better place for you to grow up than your mom and me. And I was right, wasn't I? My brother checked in once in a while. Your mom never knew that.

I knew your mom, your beautiful mom, would find someone better, that you would get a real man, a good man, for a dad. So I left. It sounds like the worst thing ever, but I did it so I would never hurt you.

***

He wished he'd written this on the computer. It was all wrong, and he wanted to rewrite it. But it wasn't the kind of letter to write on a computer. This, writing with his hand, was as close a human contact as he'd had with her in her twelve years.

He remembered that week she was born: he was supposed to check in at home every few hours, instead he disappeared in drink and speedballs. He wanted it to be over, but he didn't know what he wanted to be over. He remembered clearing out the apartment, finding a hotel room. He remembered getting so drunk. He remembered fucking that girl. He remembered how hot she was, and he cried. He hated himself. He hated himself then, before then, and now.

***

I didn't have the guts to tell her. I wrote a letter the day that you were born. I was in a fever those days. Hot and crazy and delusional. I wrote unfriendly things.

Truly cruel. I wanted her to hate me and forget about me and move on. I wanted her to not want me back, if she ever did. I thought she'd get the man she deserved and you'd grow up in this perfect family. I promised I'd let you both have your lives in peace. I don't know why she never found someone else. But my guess would be that she wanted you all to herself, and herself all for you.

When you were three months old she moved to Saskatoon. I never knew why, and I don't really know much since. It was hard to keep my promise, I wanted to talk to her, to hear you. But that was selfish. I kept my promise to let you both live and get over me and not hurt you, ever. When I got straight finally, and could work again, I sent cheques every month. That was our only communication. She never asked for them. I don't say that to try and claim that was anything good of me, I just mean to be honest and tell you the whole story.

I've been torn my whole life, over her and you. I wanted Jen to move on, but I never moved on. I became worse for a while, but then I got better. I probably wouldn't be writing now if I didn't think I were better. At least for that.

I'm sorry you lost your mom. I'm sorry you didn't have a dad. I'm sorry your real dad was a failure to you. If there's anything I can do, if you want to have any communication with me, I'm here.

Wow. That was a lot to write, and I bet a lot to read. So what else? I told you I play guitar. I have a brother. I don't sculpt or paint anymore. I would if you wanted to learn or just liked to do it with someone.

***

He paused a long time before signing his name. He wanted to write 'love' but it was selfish. He wished he could write 'Dad' but he knew he never would, not in his life. He wrote, 'Sincerely, Ryan' then wrote his email, his address, and his phone number.

He stared at the name. Sincerely, Ryan. He remembered the same signature on the other letter. He could see it! Scribbled by hand. He hated that memory. The letter, the writing of it. Jen's mom finding him at the apartment. Not to bring his ass to the hospital. Nope. To give him money to go away, and threats to make sure. In all the awfulness, he hated to remember that - the most money he ever got was to go away. So he got the hotel, and wrote the letter, and fucked the girl. He obliterated his mind, his self, in drink and drugs until he found himself in the bus station in Kelowna. His first stop.

He didn't blame them, they were right. As much as he hated that money then, and wanted to burn it, throw it away, drink it away, or flush it down the toilet, he couldn't have left Vancouver without that money. He wondered if Jen ever knew. That was the one thing he'd wanted her to know most, but how selfish was that?

He was suddenly aware that he could hear the TV upstairs. How had he not noticed it? He somehow knew it had not just been turned on, but had been there behind his thoughts the whole time.

He crumpled up the letter and threw it in the trash bin. He fell down in the corner, running his hand through his thin grey hair and crying.

***

There was no return address on the letter. Her grandmother gave it to her in the quiet kitchen. Her grandmother assumed it was some condolence, and she watched to see as the

137

girl opened it. Instead, the girl left the table and walked up to her mother's old room where she was staying. She opened the envelope and took out the small notepad pages that had been crumpled and then flattened and folded. She saw the first line.

She sat down on her mom's bed and kept reading.

The End

Locked in the Trunk of a Car, 2nd Variation

(album: Fully Completely)

What I live in is a kind of darkness, in which not just sight but every sense is cut off. You're conscious, you don't fall asleep, but there's no outside experience that enters your mind, alters your thoughts. I don't really know if this can even be described as consciousness - all I'm conscious of is my own thinking. I think, therefore I am. Am I? Without the senses, there's nothing. No time passes - no clock, no day and night, no pulse. No surroundings, no air, no smell of it, no feel of it against the skin, pulling on the hair, no sound of it brushing or whistling around me. No air, perhaps no me. Without a world to exist in, what is my existence?

Losing track of time scares me. It messes with the mind. Time defines experience - things happen in an order, they fill up a certain space. Without that, you can't know anything. You can't even rest, or take a break from thinking. There's no time to rest in. It messes with you. After a while, you don't know what was real, what was just thought, what was repeated, or if you're in some kind of... loop. Imagine being lost at sea, a black night, treading water in the open ocean. You don't even know what could be just below your feet. Imagine if somehow this aloneness could last forever. I scream. I have to. That is, I think I scream. I don't feel anything, muscle, mouth, wind in my pipes. But I wouldn't hear it if it were there either, so there's no proof either way.

If you close your eyes and move your arm, for example, can you really feel it, or do you just think you feel it moving because you know you're moving it? I don't remember actually, but I don't feel anything now. Could I be encapsulated in something? Maybe you get so used to being in the same position, stuck in something blocking everything, you get used to the feeling, and feeling it all over you eventually begins to feel like - like nothing.

I know I've thought this before.

I can't feel my belly, I don't know if I'm hungry.

I think I'm dead. I don't remember how I got here; it's hard to know. I don't know how old I am and how long it's been like this. That's how it messes with you, you don't know if this just started or if it's all you ever had - without time, everything that I'm not thinking right now kind of fades. I think this must be death. But I wonder if this is everything? Am I the only one like this? Is everyone that's ever died all just stuck like this, by themselves? Or is this a special punishment? Have I done something? Are there any others like me? Is there some time this will end, when something else will happen, when I'll feel something else? When I'll know what is outside of me? Did I ever even live or have I made that all up?

I always thought, at least when you're dead, you know. You know what's out there. All the questions get answered. There's either something or nothing. If there's nothing, then it doesn't matter, there's nothing, and no more You to worry about it. If there's something, then you're going to know what it is. But I don't know anything. Why? Is there a reason I'm not allowed to know? Would it be better for them if I don't understand?

I know I've thought this before.
Let me out. LET ME OUT!

The End

Some of these stories are also available as ebooks. Check my website or join my mailing list for updates - plus free ebooks and advance looks at new work.

Mailing list: www.bit.ly/davidsachsnews

Website: www.davidsachs.com

Picture credits: Hip

 Calgary, AB, CANADA. 1st Aug, 2016. © Baden Roth/ZUMA Wire/Alamy Live News

 Mar 26, 2007 - San Francisco, CA © Jerome Brunet/ZUMA Press/ Alamy

 Sep 15, 2006; Austin, TX, USA; Jerome Brunet/ZUMA Press/Alamy

 Victoria, B.C., Canada July 22, 2016. RE REUTERS/Kevin Light/ Alamy

 Toronto, ON Canada Day, July 01, 2011; Igor Vidyashev / Alamy

 Sep 15, 2006; Austin, TX, USA; Jerome Brunet/ZUMA Press/ Alamy

 Hamilton, ON, Canada. 16th Aug, 2016. Brent Perniac/AdMedia/ ZUMA Wire/ Alamy Live News

 Toronto, Ontario, Canada. 10th Aug, 2016. Igor Vidyashev/ZUMA Wire/Alamy Live News

 Toronto, Ontario, Canada. 19th Feb, 2015. Igor Vidyashev/ZUMA Wire/Alamy Live News

 Toronto on Canada Day, July 01, 2011 Igor Vidyashev / Alamy

 Sep 15, 2006; Austin, TX, USA; Jerome Brunet/ ZUMA Press, Inc. / Alamy

 Kingston, Ont., on May 25, 2016. Lars Hagberg / Alamy

Picture credits: Canadiana

Introducing **THE FLOOD**, *the debut novel from David Sachs*

For three years, Travis Cooke has dreamed of reuniting his family, but not like this.

When the Flood hit, America's East Coast was evacuated by every means possible. Hours later, the Festival of the Waves, a cruise ship assisting in the rescue lies dead in the water: no power, no communications, and nowhere near enough food. Thousands of refugees on board, including Travis, his-ex-wife, and their young son, find themselves alone in a big ocean.

Now, the escapees from the Flood face a new challenge - survive until rescue comes - and a journey into human darkness and heroism begins. Desperate to protect his family as the panic rises, Travis finds behind each door an unexpected new side to the Festival, but no way out. How far will he go?

For those that escaped the Flood, the nightmare is just beginning.

Buy it here: www.bit.ly/thefloodamazon

Praise for David Sachs' debut novel, The Flood

"Sachs keeps the story moving full-steam-ahead, balancing his fleshed-out portraits of memorable characters with visceral action scenes... ...An engaging and ultimately devastating disaster novel."
-Kirkus Reviews Recommendation

"An epic thriller and a remarkable work of art."
-Matthew Mather, bestselling author of CyberStorm

***

From Amazon's 5-star reviews:

*

"Stands alone and stood out."

*

"Well written, well plotted, fast moving, with complex characters. I was totally engrossed in the story from the start and found it hard to put down."

*

"A gripping page turner of a story that keeps you guessing chapter after chapter."

*

"Felt like I'd been through the wringer by the time I was done. Will stay with me for a long time."

ABOUT THE AUTHOR

Award-winning writer DAVID SACHS lives in Chelsea, Quebec (Canada), in the woods of Parc du la Gatineau. His first novel, The Flood, has been a bestseller and was finalist for ForeWord Review's Indy Book of the Year. He is a long time feature writer for magazines and newspapers, writing on politics, culture, society and the outdoors, covering everything from anti-globalization riots to Amazonian shamanism, and from homelessness to hitchhiking. His feature film, The Last Party, is in development with Bunk 11 Pictures.

He is a father, an avid outdoorsman and rugby old boy, and a former physicist and Canadian Forces reserves officer. David is an organizer for international development, social services and political groups, and a deadly boogie woogie piano player.

He first saw the Hip around '89 or '90 , at Lansdowne Park, in Ottawa.

http://www.davidsachs.com
david@davidsachs.com
@TheDavidSachs

Thanks

I'd like to thank the Tragically Hip for making great music for all these years and being such a large part of our lives. Canadians know.

CPSIA information can be obtained
at www.ICGtesting.com
Printed in the USA
LVHW072251161218
600167LV00017BA/70/P